William Shakespeare's Richard II: A Retelling in Prose

David Bruce

Published by David Bruce, 2022.

WILLIAM SHAKESPEARE'S RICHARD II: A RETELLING IN PROSE

First edition. July 28, 2022.

ISBN: 979-8201045333

Written by David Bruce.

Table of Contents

Dedication

Dedicated to My Sister Brenda

Brenda wrote, "During COVID and when visitors were restricted from visiting their loved one in the assisted-living facility I worked at, a patient mentioned to me how much she liked spaghetti during a late-night conversation we had. She was a night owl like me. Her name was Dee. I called her "Gerdy." Then she would say, "Dirty Gerdy," and we'd laugh. Anyway, on my way to work I bought two spaghetti meals from Olive Garden. I left for work early that night. I went to work, set up outlet dinners in the dining room, went to her room and wheeled her down to the dining room where we had dinner together. At that time, the residents weren't leaving their room and had their meals alone in their room. It was nighttime and everyone was already in bed, so I didn't see a problem. She was so grateful and had enough food for three more meals. It was such a simple gesture, but during that time it meant so much to her and for me."

Brenda once bought a newspaper at a gas station on Thanksgiving and tipped the female employee $5, and the employee cried.

Brenda wrote, "I do remember that. I also remember when George tipped a TeeJays waitress $100, and she cried. Our family does a lot of good deeds all the time: I unload people's grocery carts when the people are in those electric scooters. If they are alone with a few groceries, I'll leave cash for the cashier to pay for the groceries. I've had a lot of good deeds done to me when I didn't have a lot of money. It feels good to pay it forward."

She added, "I just have one more thing to add and then I'm done. I've had a lot of people in my life do good deeds for me when I was at a low point on my life. I was at a low point for a very long time. David, you know what you've done for me, and I can never thank you enough. Martha paid for antibiotics for me when I had strep throat and didn't have money. Rosa bought me groceries. Carla has done so much, and she had us over for Easter just after Chad died. When I say US, I mean all of my kids. She was so sick and ended up at the Emergency Room that same night. Frank gave me a car. And George buys my gas for me whenever he's in Florida. And Mom and Dad were good people. I had a lot of good influences in my life that made me be a good person. At least I hope I'm a good person. I try to be someone Mom and Dad would be proud of."

***

The doing of good deeds is important. As a free person, you can choose to live your life as a good person or as a bad person. To be a good person, do good deeds. To be a bad person, do bad deeds. If you do good deeds, you will become good. If you do bad deeds, you will become bad. To become the person you want to be, act as if you already are that kind of person. Each of us chooses what kind of person we will become. To become a good person, do the things a good person does. To become a bad person, do the things a bad person does. The opportunity to take action to become the kind of person you want to be is yours.

Educate Yourself

Read Like A Wolf Eats

Be Excellent to Each Other

Books Then, Books Now, Books Forever

***

In this retelling, as in all my retellings, I have tried to make the work of literature accessible to modern readers who may lack the knowledge about mythology, religion, and history that the literary work's contemporary audience had.

Do you know a language other than English? If you do, I give you permission to translate this book, copyright your translation, publish or self-publish it, and keep all the royalties for yourself. (Do give me credit, of course, for the original retelling.)

I would like to see my retellings of classic literature used in schools, so I give permission to the country of Finland (and all other countries) to give copies of this book to all students forever. I also give permission to the state of Texas (and all other states) to give copies of this book to all students forever. I also give permission to all teachers to give copies of this book to all students forever.

Teachers need not actually teach my retellings. Teachers are welcome to give students copies of my eBooks as background material. For example, if they are teaching Homer's *Iliad* and *Odyssey*, teachers are welcome to give students copies of my *Virgil's* Aeneid: *A Retelling in Prose* and tell students, "Here's another ancient epic you may want to read in your spare time."

CAST OF CHARACTERS

MALE CHARACTERS

King Richard II; his father was the late Edward of Woodstock, known as The Black Prince

Henry, surnamed Bolingbroke, Duke of Hereford, son of John of Gaunt; afterwards King Henry IV

Uncles of King Richard II

John of Gaunt, Duke of Lancaster; father of Henry Bolingbroke; he was called John of Gaunt because Gaunt was his birthplace; in modern English his birthplace is spelled Ghent; Ghent is in Belgium

Edmund of Langley, Duke of York; uncle to both King Richard II and Henry Bolingbroke

All of King Richard II's other uncles are dead at the beginning of Shakespeare's play

Supporters of King Richard II

Sir John Bushy, friend of King Richard II

Sir John Bagot, friend of King Richard II

Sir Henry Green, friend of King Richard II

Earl of Salisbury

Lord Berkeley

Bishop of Carlisle

Abbot of Westminster

Sir Stephen Scroop

Captain of a band of Welshmen

Supporters of Henry Bolingbroke, Duke of Hereford

Earl of Northumberland

Henry Percy, son to Northumberland; in *1 Henry IV*, young Henry Percy has acquired the nickname "Hotspur"

Lord Ross

Lord Willoughby

Officials in Trial by Combat

Lord Marshal

First Herald

Second Herald

Other Male Characters

Duke of Aumerle, son to the Duke of York; another of his titles is Earl of Rutland

Thomas Mowbray, Duke of Norfolk

Duke of Surrey

Lord Fitzwater

Sir Pierce of Exton

FEMALE CHARACTERS

Queen to King Richard II

Duchess of York

Duchess of Gloucester

Two ladies attending on the Queen

MINOR CHARACTERS

Lords, Heralds, Officers, Soldiers, Head Gardener, two Assistant Gardeners, Jail Keeper, Messenger, Groom, and other Attendants

SCENE

England and Wales

NOTA BENE

See "Appendix A: Brief Historical Background" if you need a very brief refresher on English history.

King Richard II's reign began on 21 June 1377; he was deposed on 30 September 1399 and then murdered on 14 February 1400.

King Richard II and Henry Bolingbroke were first cousins. They shared the same grandfather: King Edward III. Their fathers were brothers, and so each man's father was the other man's uncle.

The action of this book begins in 1398; the previous year the Duke of Gloucester had been killed. The Duke of Gloucester was the brother of John of Gaunt and the uncle of both King Richard II and Henry Bolingbroke. The action of this book ends in 1400.

CHAPTER 1

— 1.1 —

At Windsor Castle, King Richard II talked with John of Gaunt. Other nobles and attendants were present.

King Richard II said, "Old John of Gaunt, time-honored Duke of Lancaster, have you, according to your oath and bond, brought here Henry Bolingbroke, Duke of Hereford, your bold son, to make good his boisterous and violent recent accusation, which then our lack of leisure would not let us hear, against the Duke of Norfolk, Thomas Mowbray?"

"I have, my liege," replied John of Gaunt.

"Tell me, moreover, have you questioned him to find out if he accuses the Duke of Norfolk on account of ancient hatred toward him, or worthily, as a good subject should, on some known ground of treachery in him?"

"As near as I could find out by questioning him on that topic, he makes the accusation on account of some apparent and obvious danger seen in the Duke of Norfolk that is aimed at your highness, and not because of long-standing malice and hatred."

"Then call them into our presence," King Richard II said, using the royal plural. "We ourselves will hear the accuser and the accused — face to face, and frowning brow to brow — freely speak. High-stomached — proud and stubborn — are they both, and full of ire; in rage they are deaf as the sea, and as hasty as fire."

Henry Bolingbroke, Duke of Hereford, and Thomas Mowbray, Duke of Norfolk, entered the room.

Henry Bolingbroke said to King Richard II, "May many years of happy days befall you, my gracious sovereign, my most loving liege!"

Thomas Mowbray said to the King, "May each day always better the previous day's happiness, until the Heavens, envying Earth's good fortune, add an immortal title to your crown!"

"We thank you both," King Richard II replied, "yet one of you is only flattering us, as well appears by the reason you come here — namely to accuse each other of high treason.

"Henry, my cousin of Hereford, what accusation do you bring against the Duke of Norfolk, Thomas Mowbray?"

"First, let Heaven be the witness to my speech!" Henry Bolingbroke said. "In the devotion of a subject's love, feeling concern for the precious safety of my Prince, and free from other misbegotten hate, I come as accuser into this Princely presence.

"Now, Thomas Mowbray, I turn to you. Mark well what I say to you; for what I speak my body shall make good upon this Earth, or my divine soul shall answer it in Heaven. I will fight you and prove by defeating and killing you that you are guilty of what I accuse you.

"You are a traitor and a miscreant, too highborn to be these things and too bad to live, since the more beautiful and crystal-clear the sky is, the uglier seem the clouds that in it fly.

"Once more, the more to aggravate the mark of your disgrace, I stuff down your throat the name of a foul traitor, and I wish, if it pleases my sovereign, before I move, to prove with sword drawn in righteous cause to prove that what I say is true."

Thomas Mowbray replied, "Let not my cool, calm words here make anyone accuse me of lacking zeal. The trial of a woman's war, the bitter clamor of two eager tongues, a battle fought only with words, cannot arbitrate this dispute between us two. The blood is hot that must be cooled for this. We must fight and spill blood on the ground.

"Yet I cannot boast of possessing such tame patience as to be hushed and to say nothing at all.

"First, the fair reverence of your highness — my respect for you, King Richard II, who are a blood relative to Henry Bolingbroke — curbs me from giving reins and spurs to my free speech, which otherwise would posthaste return these terms of treason and stuff them redoubled down his throat.

"Setting aside his high blood's royalty, thereby letting him be no kinsman to my liege, I defy him, and I spit at him. I call him a slanderous coward and a villain, and to prove that what I say is true I would allow him odds, and meet him in man-to-man combat, even if I were obliged to run on foot all the way to the frozen ridges of the Alps, or any other uninhabitable ground where an Englishman has dared to set his foot.

"In the meantime let *this* defend my loyalty," Thomas Mowbray said as he put his hand on the hilt of his sword. "I swear by all my hopes of attaining Heaven that most falsely he lies."

Henry Bolingbroke threw his glove on the ground. The glove was his gage, a challenge to fight. If Thomas Mowbray picked up the gage, the two were obliged to fight.

Henry Bolingbroke said, "Pale trembling coward, there I throw my gage. I renounce here the kindred of the King, and I lay aside my high blood's royalty. I say that fear of me, not respect for my being related to the King, makes you hold back from fighting me. You say that you respect the blood of the King — well, now that I have renounced my royal blood, you have no reason not to fight me.

"If guilty dread has left you so much strength as to take up my honor's pawn, then stoop and pick up my gage. By that gage and all the other rites of knighthood, I will make good against you, arm against arm, what I have spoken, before you can devise even worse crimes to commit."

Thomas Mowbray picked up the gage and said, "I take it up, and by that sword that gently tapped me on my shoulder when I was knighted, I swear that I'll answer your challenge in any fair degree or chivalrous design of knightly trial. And when I mount my horse to fight you, may I not dismount alive from my horse, if I am a traitor or if I fight for an unjust cause!"

King Richard II said to Henry Bolingbroke, his first cousin, "What crime does our cousin charge that Mowbray is responsible for? It must be great if it will possess us of even as much as a thought of evil in him."

"Pay attention to what I say," Henry Bolingbroke replied. "My life shall prove that what I say is true. Mowbray received eight thousand nobles to pay as lendings — advances of pay — for your highness' soldiers, but he retained that money and used it for improper employments, like a false, treacherous traitor and injurious villain.

"In addition, I say and will in battle prove, either here or elsewhere to the furthest border that ever was surveyed by English eye, that for these past eighteen years since the Peasants' Revolt of 1381 all the treasons plotted and contrived in this land stem from false Mowbray, who is their first head and spring."

The Duke of Gloucester had been murdered while in the custody of Thomas Mowbray. Some people in this society believed that King Richard II had ordered the death of the Duke of Gloucester and that Thomas Mowbray, after delaying for three weeks, had ordered people who served him to carry out the order. The Duke of Gloucester was the uncle of both Henry Bolingbroke and King Richard II.

Referring to this murder, Henry Bolingbroke continued, "Further I say and further I will maintain upon his bad life to make all this good, that he plotted the Duke of Gloucester's death, tempted his soon-believing adversaries, and subsequently, like a traitor coward, sluiced out the Duke of Gloucester's innocent soul through streams of blood. This blood, like the blood of Abel, who sacrificed lambs to God and then was murdered by Cain, whose sacrifice of crops was not as well regarded by God, cries, even from the tongueless caverns of the earth, to me for justice and rough chastisement, and, by the glorious worth of my descent, this arm shall do it before this life is spent."

The story of Abel and Cain is told in Genesis 4. In Genesis 4:12, we read, "The Lord said, 'What have you done? Listen! Your brother's blood cries out to me from the ground.'"

King Richard II said, "To how high a height the resolution of Henry Bolingbroke soars!

"Thomas Mowbray of Norfolk, what do you say to this?"

"Oh, let my sovereign turn away his face and bid his ears be deaf for a little while until I have told this disgrace to his blood relatives how God and good men hate so foul a liar."

"Mowbray, our eyes and ears are impartial," King Richard II said. "If Henry Bolingbroke were my brother, or even my Kingdom's heir — although as it is, he is only my father's brother's son — but now, by the reverence due to my scepter and my majesty, I make a vow that such neighbor nearness to our sacred blood shall not privilege him, nor shall his close blood relationship to me make the unstooping firmness of my upright soul biased in his favor."

Richard II believed that Kings are supposed to stoop — bow — to no one except God.

King Richard II continued, "Henry Bolingbroke is our subject, Mowbray, and so are you. I grant you permission to speak freely and without fear."

Thomas Mowbray said, "Then, Bolingbroke, I say that as low as to your heart, through the perfidious passage of your throat, you lie. Three parts of that money I received for Calais I duly disbursed to his highness' soldiers. The other part I retained with King Richard II's consent because my sovereign liege was in my debt because of an unpaid balance of a dear — both expensive and loving — account. I paid out my own money when recently I went to France to fetch King Richard II's Queen. Now swallow down that lie."

King Richard II had married Isabella of Valois.

Thomas Mowbray continued, "As for the Duke of Gloucester's death, I did not slay him, but to my own disgrace I neglected my sworn duty in that case.

"As for you, my noble John of Gaunt, Duke of Lancaster, you who are the honorable father to my foe, I once lay an ambush for your life. That is a trespass that vexes my grieving soul, but before I last received the sacrament I confessed my sin and expressly begged for your grace's pardon, and I hope I had it.

"That is my fault. As for the other things I am accused of, they issue from the rancor of a villain, a cowardly and most degenerate traitor, and I boldly will defend myself against those charges."

He threw down his glove and said, "I in turn hurl down my gage upon this overweening and arrogant traitor's foot, and I will prove myself a loyal gentleman even in the best blood chambered in his bosom. I will spill the blood of his heart to prove that I am a loyal gentleman.

"Most heartily I pray that your highness will quickly assign a day for our trial by combat."

Both Henry Bolingbroke and Thomas Mowbray had picked up the other's gage.

"Wrath-kindled gentlemen, be ruled by me," King Richard II said. "Let's purge this choler without letting blood."

In this society, physicians sometimes treated illnesses by bleeding. The physician would make shallow incisions in veins and bleed the patient.

Using the royal plural, King Richard II continued, "This we prescribe, although we are no physician. Deep malice makes too deep incision. Forget and forgive; come to terms and be agreed to be reconciled. Our doctors say this is no month to bleed."

In this society, physicians believed that some months were more favorable than others for bleeding.

Using the royal plural, King Richard II said to John of Gaunt, "Good uncle, let this end where it began. We'll calm the Duke of Norfolk; you calm your son."

John of Gaunt said, "To be a peacemaker shall be suitable for my age. Throw down, my son, the Duke of Norfolk's gage."

King Richard II said, "And, Duke of Norfolk, throw down Bolingbroke's gage."

Henry Bolingbroke did not throw down Mowbray's gage. Nor did Mowbray throw down Bolingbroke's gage.

John of Gaunt said, "When, Harry, when will you do what I tell you to do? Filial obedience bids I should not bid again. A dutiful son would have already done what I told you to do."

King Richard II said, "Norfolk, we order you to throw down Henry Bolingbroke's gage; there is no alternative."

Thomas Mowbray knelt and said, "Myself I throw, dread sovereign, at your foot. My life you shall command, but not my shame. The one my duty owes to you, but my fair name, a name that will live on after I am dead and in my grave, to dark dishonor's use you shall not have. I am disgraced, accused, and publicly treated with infamy here. I am pierced to the soul with the poisoned spear of slander, and no balm can cure that except the heart's-blood of the man who uttered these poisoned words against me."

"Rage must be withstood," King Richard II said. "Give me Henry Bolingbroke's gage. Lions make leopards tame. Kings make nobles tame."

"Yes, lions make leopards tame, but they cannot change the leopard's spots," Mowbray said. "Just take away my shame, and I will resign my challenge and take back my gage."

A spot is a stain, aka sin or crime. Mowbray may have been saying that if King Richard II would admit that he had ordered the death of the Duke of Gloucester, then Mowbray would take back his gage and his challenge.

Mowbray continued, "My dear, dear lord, the purest treasure mortal times afford is spotless reputation. Take that away, and men are only gilded loam or painted clay."

According to Genesis, God created men out of dust. Take away a man's spotless reputation, and all that is left is dust that has been covered with gilt or paint.

Mowbray continued, "A jewel in a ten-times-barred-up chest is like a bold spirit in a loyal breast. My honor is my life; both grow in one — they are intertwined. Take honor from me, and my life is done. So then, my dear liege, let me put my honor to the test. In defending honor I live, and for honor I will die."

King Richard II said to Henry Bolingbroke, "Cousin, give up your challenge; you begin the peace-making process."

"Oh, may God keep my soul from such deep sin!" Henry Bolingbroke said. "Shall I seem crestfallen and humbled in my father's sight? Or with fear appropriate to a pale beggar discredit my high birth before this brazen dastardly coward? Before my tongue shall wound my honor with such feeble wrong, or sound so base a truce, my teeth shall tear the slavish instrument of recanting fear, and I will spit my bleeding tongue with its high disgrace where shame finds harbor — I will spit my tongue in Mowbray's face."

King Richard II said, "We were not born to beseech, but to command, which since we cannot do to make you friends, be ready, as your lives shall answer for it if you are not ready, at Coventry, upon Saint Lambert's day — September 17 — in this year of 1398. There shall your swords and lances arbitrate the swelling difference of your deep-rooted hate. Since we cannot reconcile you, we shall see the justice of God designate which of you shall be the victor and therefore is in the right.

"Lord Marshal, command our officers at arms to be ready to manage these home — as opposed to foreign — disturbances."

In his house in London, John of Gaunt and the Duchess of Gloucester, whose husband had been murdered at King Richard II's order, talked together.

John of Gaunt said, "Alas, the blood I shared with my brother Thomas of Woodstock, the Duke of Gloucester, urges me more than your exclamations to stir and take action against the butchers of his life! But since correction lies in the hands of him who committed the crime — the King's hands — we cannot avenge the crime, and so we leave revenge to the will of Heaven. God, when He sees the right time and the ripe hours on Earth, will rain hot vengeance on such offenders' heads."

The Duchess of Gloucester said, "Doesn't brotherhood find in you a sharper spur? Has love in your old blood no living fire? King Edward III had seven sons, and you yourself are one. Those seven sons were like seven vials of his sacred blood, or seven beautiful branches springing from one root. Some of those seven are dried by nature's course; they have died. Some of those branches were cut by the Destinies — the Fates who spin, weave, measure, and cut the thread of life.

"But Thomas of Woodstock, my dear lord, my life, my Duke of Gloucester, who was one vial full of King Edward III's sacred blood, one flourishing branch of his most royal root, is cracked, and all the precious liquor spilt. He is hacked down and his summer leaves are all faded, by hatred's hand and murder's bloody axe.

"Ah, Gaunt, his blood was yours! That bed, that womb, that stuff, that same mold that fashioned you made him a man; and although you live and breathe, yet you are slain in him. You consent in some large measure to your father's death, in that you see your wretched brother die, who was the model of your father's life.

"Don't call it Christian patience, Gaunt; it is despair and desperation — a sin. Despair is loss of hope. Christian patience is forbearance and self-control; it is Christian long-suffering — waiting patiently for God to act.

"In allowing thus your brother to be slaughtered, you show the naked, defenseless pathway to your own life, and you teach stern murder how to butcher you. That which in mean men we entitle patience is pale cold cowardice when it appears in noble breasts.

"What shall I say? To safeguard your own life, the best way is to avenge my Gloucester's death."

"God's is the quarrel," John of Gaunt replied. "God's substitute, His deputy anointed in His sight, has caused the death of the Duke of Gloucester. That substitute is King Richard II, who was crowned in the sight of God in the coronation ceremony at Westminster Abbey. All Kings, good or bad, are God's deputies. If King Richard II caused Gloucester's death wrongfully, let Heaven revenge it, for I may never lift an angry arm against the minister of God."

"To whom then, alas, may I complain?" the Duchess of Gloucester asked.

"To God, the widow's champion and defense."

"Why, then, I will. Farewell, old Gaunt. You go to Coventry, there to behold our kinsman the Duke of Hereford fight deadly Mowbray.

"Oh, may my husband's wrongs sit on Hereford's spear, so that it may enter the butcher Mowbray's breast! Or, if misfortune miss the first charge in the man-to-man combat, may Mowbray's sins sit so heavy in his bosom that they break his foaming courser's back, and throw the rider headlong in the combat arena, a captive coward to my cousin Hereford!

"Farewell, old Gaunt. Your at one time brother's wife with her companion, Grief, must end her life."

"Sister-in-law, farewell," John of Gaunt replied. "I must go to Coventry. May as much good stay with you as goes with me!"

"Yet one word more," the Duchess of Gloucester said. "Grief rebounds from where it falls, not with its empty hollowness, but with its weight. It rebounds because it is so heavy and returns to the mourner.

"I take my leave before I have begun, for sorrow does not end when it seems to be done.

"Commend me to your brother, Edmund of Langley, the Duke of York.

"Well, that is all — no, do not yet depart. Although this is all, do not so quickly go. I shall remember more things to say. Tell the Duke of York — ah, what? — with all good speed at Plashy visit me."

Plashy was the home of the Gloucester family in Essex.

The Duchess of Gloucester continued, "Alas, and what shall good old York see there but empty rooms and undecorated walls since the tapestries have been taken down while I am away. What shall good old York see there but unpeopled rooms where servants should be doing their work, and untrodden stones? And what should old York hear there for his welcome except my groans?

"Therefore convey my greetings to him, but let him not come there to seek the sorrow that dwells everywhere.

"Desolate, desolate, I will go there and die. My weeping eyes now take their last leave of you."

On this Saint Lambert's day — 17 September 1398 — the lists — the area prepared for combat — had been prepared at Coventry for the combat between Henry Bolingbroke and Mowbray. The duel would decide which man was honorable; people believed that God would help the honorable man defeat the dishonorable man in this fight to the death.

The Lord Marshal and the Duke of Aumerle spoke together.

The Lord Marshal asked, "My Lord Aumerle, is Harry Bolingbroke, Duke of Hereford, armed?"

"Yes, at all points he is fully armed, and he longs to enter into the fighting arena."

The Lord Marshal said, "The Duke of Norfolk, full of spirit and bold, waits only for the summons of the accuser's trumpet."

The Duke of Aumerle replied, "Why, then, the champions are prepared, and I am waiting for nothing except his majesty's approach."

The trumpets sounded, and King Richard II entered with John of Gaunt, Bushy, Bagot, Green, and others. They sat, and Thomas Mowbray, fully armed, entered with his herald. Mowbray was the defendant in this trial by arms.

King Richard II said, "Lord Marshal, demand of yonder champion the cause of his arrival here in arms. Ask him his name and orderly proceed to make him swear to the justice of his cause."

The Lord Marshal said to Mowbray, "In God's name and the King's, say who you are and why you have come here thus knightly clad in arms, say against what man you have come here to fight, and say what are your quarrel and cause of complaint with that man. Speak truly, on your knighthood and your oath, and may God and your valor protect you in accordance with the justice of your cause."

Knights identified themselves as part of the ritual. They were wearing helmets with the visors down and in some cases would not be recognized. Also, one of the rules of chivalry was that knights were under no obligation to fight those challengers who were not knights.

"My name is Thomas Mowbray, Duke of Norfolk, and I have come here engaged by my oath — which God forbid a knight should violate! — both to defend my loyalty and truth to God, my King, and my descendants against the Duke of Hereford who accuses me and, by the grace of God and this my arm, to prove, in defending myself, that he is a traitor to my God, my King, and me, and as I fight for the truth, may Heaven defend me!"

The trumpets sounded, and Henry Bolingbroke, the accuser of Mowbray, entered the combat arena fully armed, accompanied by a herald.

King Richard II said, "Marshal, ask yonder knight in arms both who he is and why he comes here thus armed in plate armor in the habiliments of war, and formally, according to our law, take an oath from him about the justice of his cause."

The Lord Marshal asked, "What is your name? And why have you come here before King Richard II in his royal lists? Against whom have you come? And what's your quarrel? Speak like a true knight, so that Heaven may defend you!"

"I am Harry of Hereford, Lancaster, and Derby," Henry Bolingbroke replied.

He called himself Lancaster because he was the heir to the Duke of Lancaster. He was also the Duke of Hereford and the Earl of Derby.

He continued, "I stand here in arms ready to prove, by God's grace and my body's valor, in this combat arena, against Thomas Mowbray, Duke of Norfolk, that he is a traitor, foul and dangerous, to God of Heaven, King Richard II, and to me, and as I fight for the truth, may Heaven defend me!"

The Lord Marshal said, "On pain of death, no person shall be so bold or foolhardy as to interfere in the combat arena, except the Marshal and such officers as are appointed to direct this fair undertaking."

"Lord Marshal," Henry Bolingbroke said, "let me kiss my sovereign's hand, and bow my knee before his majesty, for Mowbray and I are like two men who vow a long and weary pilgrimage. Then let us take a ceremonious leave and loving farewell of our many friends."

The Lord Marshal said to King Richard II, "The accuser greets your highness in all duty, and he requests to kiss your hand and take his leave."

"We will descend and enfold him in our arms," King Richard II said, coming down from his chair of state, which was on a platform, and hugging Henry Bolingbroke, his first cousin.

He added, "Cousin of Hereford, to that extent that your cause is right, so be your fortune in this royal fight! If your cause is just, then win. If your cause is unjust, then die. Farewell, my blood. If today you shed your blood, I am permitted to lament you, but not to revenge your death. If you die, Mowbray has proven that your cause is unjust, and revenging your death would be unjust."

"Oh, let no noble eye drop a profane tear for me, if I am gored with Mowbray's spear," Henry Bolingbroke replied. "As confidently as against a bird the falcon takes flight, I with Mowbray fight. My loving lord, I take my leave of you.

"I also take my leave of you, my noble cousin, Lord Aumerle. I am not sick, although I have to do with death; instead, I am strong, young, and cheerfully drawing breath.

"Lo, as at English feasts, at which sweet things are served last, so I greet the sweetest, most delicious, and daintiest last, to make the end most sweet."

He then said to his father, John of Gaunt, "Oh, you, the Earthly author of my blood, whose youthful spirit, in me reborn, with a twofold vigor lifts me up to reach out for victory above my head, add tested strength to my armor with your prayers, and with your blessings steel and strengthen my lance's point so that it may pierce Mowbray's armor as if it were made of wax, and polish anew the name of John of Gaunt through the vigorous behavior of his son."

John of Gaunt replied, "May God make you prosperous because your cause is good! Be swift like lightning in the execution, and let your blows, doubly redoubled, fall like stupefying thunder on the helmet of your adverse pernicious enemy. Rouse up your youthful blood, be valiant, and live."

"I rely for success on my innocence and the help of Saint George, the patron saint of England," Henry Bolingbroke said.

Thomas Mowbray said, "However God or fortune casts my lot, there lives or dies, true to King Richard II's throne, a loyal, just, and upright gentleman: myself. Never did a captive with a freer heart cast off his chains of bondage and embrace his golden uncontrolled freedom more than my dancing soul celebrates this feast of battle with my adversary.

"Most mighty liege, and my companion peers, take away from my mouth the wish of happy years. As gentle and as jocund as to an entertainment, I go to fight. Truth has a calm breast."

"Farewell, my lord," King Richard II said. "I confidently see virtue with valor lying poised and ready in your eye.

"Order the trial, Marshal, and let the combat begin."

The Lord Marshal had inspected the opponents' lances to make sure that they were the same length. Now he gave the opponents their lances.

He said, "Harry of Hereford, Lancaster, and Derby, receive your lance; and may God defend whoever has right on his side!"

"Strong as a tower in hope, I cry, 'Amen,'" Henry Bolingbroke said.

The Lord Marshal ordered an officer, "Go bear this lance to Thomas Mowbray, Duke of Norfolk."

The first herald said, "Harry of Hereford, Lancaster, and Derby, stands here for God, his sovereign and himself, on pain to be found false and cowardly, to prove that the Duke of Norfolk, Thomas Mowbray, is a traitor to his God, his King, and himself, and dares him to set forward to the fight."

The second herald said, "Here stands Thomas Mowbray, Duke of Norfolk, on pain to be found false and cowardly, both to defend himself and to prove that Henry of Hereford, Lancaster, and Derby is to God, his sovereign, and himself disloyal. Thomas Mowbray stands here courageously and with a free desire to fight, and is waiting only for the signal to begin."

The Lord Marshal said, "Sound, trumpets; and set forward, combatants."

The trumpets sounded a charge, but King Richard II threw his warder — his baton — down. This was a signal to stop the combat.

The Lord Marshal ordered, "Stop! The King has thrown his warder down."

King Richard II said, "Let them lay by their helmets and their spears, and both return back to their chairs again."

Using the royal plural, he then ordered the lords of his Council, "Withdraw with us, and let the trumpets sound until we notify these Dukes what we decree."

The trumpets made a succession of calls until the deliberation stopped.

King Richard II then said to the combatants, "Come close, and listen to what with our Council we have decided.

"Because our Kingdom's earth should not be soiled with that dear blood that it has fostered, and because our eyes hate the dire aspect of wounds plowed up with neighbors' swords in civil war, and because we think the eagle-winged pride of sky-aspiring and ambitious thoughts, with rival-hating envy, set you on to disturb our peace, which in our country's cradle draws the sweet infant breath of gentle sleep, and which would become excessively roused up with savage out-of-tune military drums, with harsh resounding trumpets' dreadful brays, and with the grating shock of wrathful iron arms — these disturbances might from our quiet confines frighten fair Peace and make us wade even in our kindred's blood — we therefore banish both of you from our territories.

"You, cousin Hereford, upon pain of losing your life, until twice five summers have enriched our fields, shall not greet again our fair dominions. Instead, for ten years you shall tread the foreign paths of banishment."

"Your will be done," Henry Bolingbroke replied. "This must be my comfort: The Sun that warms you here shall shine on me there, and the Sun's golden beams that are given to you here shall also shine on me and gild my banishment."

King Richard II said to Mowbray, "Duke of Norfolk, for you remains a heavier doom, a more serious sentence, which I with some unwillingness pronounce. The stealthy and slow hours shall not bring to an end the endless time of your dear — dire — exile. The hopeless words of 'never to return' speak I against you, upon pain of losing your life."

"This is a heavy sentence, my most sovereign liege," Mowbray replied, "and all unlooked for from your highness' mouth. I have deserved at your highness' hands a dearer merit, not so deep a wound as to be cast forth in the common air.

"The language I have learned these forty years, my native English, now I must forego. And now my tongue is of use to me no more than an unstringed viol or a harp. My tongue is as useful to me as a skillfully made musical instrument put away in its case. My tongue is as useful to me as a skillfully made musical instrument put into the hands of a person who does not know how to play a tuneful harmony. Within my mouth you have jailed my tongue. It is doubly guarded with portcullises — my teeth and lips."

A portcullis is a strong, heavy grating that can be lowered to block the entrance to a castle.

Mowbray continued, "Dull, unfeeling, barren ignorance is made my jailer to wait on me. I am too old to fawn upon a wet nurse, too far in years — too old — to be a pupil now. I cannot learn a foreign language either from a wet nurse — a servant who takes care of and breastfeeds someone else's baby and teaches it to say its first words — or from a tutor. What is your sentence then but speechless death, which robs my tongue from breathing native breath and speaking native words?"

King Richard II replied, "It does not help you to be piteously full of lamentation. After we have pronounced our sentence, complaining comes too late."

"Then thus I turn myself away from my country's light, to dwell in solemn shadows of endless night," Mowbray said, preparing to leave.

King Richard II said to him, "Return again, and take an oath with you."

Using the royal plural, he then said to both Thomas Mowbray and Henry Bolingbroke, "Lay your banished hands on our royal sword — the sword, hilt, and guard form a cross. Swear by the duty that you owe to God — now that I have banished you, you owe no duty to me — to keep this oath that we administer:

"You shall never — so help you truth and God! — embrace each other's friendship in banishment, shall never look upon each other's face, shall never write each other, greet each other again, or reconcile this frowning tempest of your home-bred hate, and shall never by premeditated plan meet to plot, contrive, or collude in any ill against us, our state, our subjects, or our land."

Henry Bolingbroke said, "I swear."

Thomas Mowbray said, "And I swear to keep all this."

Henry Bolingbroke said to Mowbray, "Duke of Norfolk, so far as I may speak to my enemy, let me say this: By this time, if the King had permitted us to fight, one of our souls had wandered in the air because it had been banished from this frail sepulcher of our flesh, as now our flesh is banished from this land. Confess your treasons before you fly from the realm. Since you have far to go, do not bear along with you the clogging burden of a guilty soul."

A clog is a weight that is attached to the leg of a prisoner to impede movement.

"No, Bolingbroke," Thomas Mowbray replied. "If I ever were a traitor, may my name be blotted from the Book of Life, and may I from Heaven be banished as I am banished from England! But what you are, God, you, and I know, and all too soon, I fear, the King shall rue what you are.

"Farewell, my liege. Now no way can I stray, unless I come back to England. All the world's my way. I can go anywhere I want except England."

Mowbray exited.

King Richard II looked at John of Gaunt, who was mourning the exile of Henry Bolingbroke.

King Richard II said, "The eyes mirror what is in the heart. Uncle, even in the mirrors of your eyes I see your grieving heart. Your sad expression has from the number of your son's banished years plucked away four years."

He said to Henry Bolingbroke, "After six frozen winters are spent and gone, return with welcome home from banishment."

Henry Bolingbroke replied, "How long a time lies in one little speech from a King! Four lagging, lingering winters and four wanton, luxuriant springs disappear with a King's small speech: Such is the breath of Kings."

John of Gaunt said, "I thank my liege because in his regard for me he shortens my son's exile by four years, but little advantage shall I reap thereby, for before the six years that my son has to spend in exile can change their Moons, making months pass, and bring their times to an end, my oil-dried lamp and my wasted-away-by-time light shall be extinct with age and endless night. My inch of taper will be burnt and done, and blindfolded death will not let me see my son. I will never see my son again; I will die before his exile is over."

"Why, uncle, you have many years to live," King Richard II said.

"But, King, you cannot give to me even a minute," John of Gaunt said. "You can shorten my days with sullen sorrow, and you can pluck nights away from me, but you cannot give me a morning. You can help time to furrow — wrinkle — me with age, but you can stop no wrinkle in time's pilgrimage. Your word is current with time for my death, but once I am dead, your Kingdom cannot buy my breath. You have the power to kill me, but once I am dead you lack the power to give me life."

"Your son is banished upon good advice," King Richard II said. "Your own tongue assented to this group verdict. Why then at our justice do you seem to frown?"

"Things sweet to taste prove in digestion to be sour," John of Gaunt said. "You urged me to express my opinion as a judge; but I had rather you would have bid me to argue like a father. Oh, if it had been a stranger and not my child I was judging, I would have been milder and glossed over his fault. I sought to avoid being accused of being biased because I was judging my son. So I advocated exile, and with this sentence I destroyed my own life. Alas, I looked for the time when some of you would say that I was too strict when I made my own son go away in exile, but you gave permission to my unwilling tongue against my will to do myself this wrong."

King Richard II said to Henry Bolingbroke, "Cousin, farewell."

He then said to John of Gaunt, "Uncle, tell your son farewell. For six years we banish him, and he shall go."

The trumpets sounded, and King Richard II and his train of attendants exited.

The Duke of Aumerle, who was loyal to King Richard II, said to Henry Bolingbroke, "Cousin, farewell. What presence must not know, from where you do remain let paper show. You won't be able to communicate with me in person, but be sure to write to me."

The Duke of Aumerle, King Richard II, and Henry Bolingbroke were all first cousins, since they were the sons of three brothers, all of whom were sons of King Edward III. The Duke of Aumerle was the son of the Duke of York.

The Lord Marshal said to Henry Bolingbroke, "My lord, no leave from you will I take, for I will ride, as far as land will let me, by your side. I will ride to the harbor with you."

Henry Bolingbroke stayed silent because of his grief at leaving England.

His father, John of Gaunt, said to him, "Oh, for what reason do you hoard your words with the result that you return no courteous sentences to your friends?"

"I have too few words to take my leave of you," Henry Bolingbroke said. "Now my tongue's duty is to be prodigal in expressing the abundant dolor of my heart."

"Your grief — cause of sorrow — is only your absence from England for a time," John of Gaunt said.

"As long as joy is absent, grief — sorrow — is present for that time," Henry Bolingbroke said.

"What are six winters? They are quickly gone."

"To men in joy, but grief makes one hour seem like ten."

"Call it a travel that you are taking for pleasure," John of Gaunt said.

"My heart will sigh when I miscall it so," Henry Bolingbroke said. "It is a travail — a forced pilgrimage."

"Think of it this way," John of Gaunt said. "The sullen, gloomy passage of your weary steps is a foil wherein you are to set the precious jewel of your home return."

A foil is a thin piece of metal set under a jewel to make it more brilliant. The foil has little value, but the jewel has great value. The time spent in exile, according to John of Gaunt, will make his son's return to England seem all the more brilliant.

"No," Henry Bolingbroke replied. "Rather, every tedious stride I make will only remind me at what a great distance away I wander from the jewels whom I love.

"Isn't it true that I must serve a long apprenticeship to foreign passages, and in the end, having again my freedom, I must boast of nothing else but that I was a journeyman to grief? I will spend time in exile, but I will gain nothing for it — except six years of serving grief."

"All places that the eye of Heaven visits are to a wise man ports and happy havens," John of Gaunt said.

A proverb stated, "A wise man makes every country his own."

He continued, "Teach your necessity to reason like this. There is no virtue like necessity.

"Don't think that the King banished you; think that you banished the King.

"Woe does the heavier sit, where it perceives it is but faintheartedly borne.

"Go, and say that I sent you forth to earn honor instead of saying that the King exiled you.

"Or suppose that a devouring pestilential plague hangs in our air and you are fleeing to a fresher, healthier climate.

"Look, whatever your soul holds dear, imagine that it lies the way you are going, and not from whence you came. Say that you are traveling to find whatever your soul holds dear.

"Imagine that the singing birds are musicians. Imagine that the grass you tread on is the King's presence chamber strewed with rushes. Imagine that the flowers are fair ladies, and your steps are no more than a delightful stately or lively dance.

"Gnarling — snarling and gnashing — sorrow has less power to bite the man who mocks it and regards it as light."

"Oh, who can hold a fire in his hand by thinking about the frosty Caucasus Mountains that separate Europe from Asia?" Henry Bolingbroke replied. "Who can cloy — satiate — the hungry edge of appetite with only the imagination of a feast? Who can wallow naked in December snow by thinking about summer's fantastic heat?

"Oh, no! The awareness of the good only gives the greater feeling to the worse. Cruel Sorrow's tooth never rankles and creates a festering wound more than when it bites and creates a sore, but does not lance it."

Some wounds do not leave an opening, meaning that any pus stays inside the body, and the wound does not heal. Lancing a wound leaves an opening that allows the pus to drain and fosters healing.

"Come, come, my son," John of Gaunt said. "I'll accompany you on your way. If I had your youth and cause, I would not delay."

"Then, England's ground, farewell," Henry Bolingbroke said. "Sweet soil, adieu. My mother, and my nurse, that bears me yet! Wherever I wander, boast of this I can: Although I am banished, I am yet a trueborn Englishman."

King Richard II was at his court. With him were Bagot and Green and the Duke of Aumerle.

"We did observe that," King Richard II said in mid-conversation.

He then said, "Cousin Aumerle, how far did you accompany high Hereford on his way?"

The word "high" was ambiguous. It could mean "highborn" or "proud and haughty."

"I accompanied high Hereford, if you call him so, only to the next highway, and there I left him," Aumerle replied.

"Tell me, what quantity of parting tears was shed?" King Richard II asked.

"Indeed, no tears were shed by me, except the north-east wind, which then blew bitterly against our faces, awakened the sleeping seepage of my eye, and so by chance I graced our hollow — insincere — parting with a tear."

"What did our cousin say when you parted from him?"

"'Farewell,' and, because my heart disdained that my tongue should so profane the word 'farewell' by saying it to Bolingbroke, my heart taught me the craftiness to counterfeit and imitate oppression of such grief that words seemed buried in my sorrow's grave. I pretended that I was so overcome with sorrow that I could not speak. Truly, if the word 'farewell' would have lengthened the hours and added years to Bolingbroke's short banishment, he would have had a volume of farewells from me, but since it would not, he had none from me."

King Richard II said, "He is our cousin, cousin."

King Richard II, the Duke of Aumerle, and Henry Bolingbroke were all first cousins.

He continued, "But when time shall call Bolingbroke home from banishment, it is doubtful whether he, our kinsman, will come back to see his friends. When his exile is ended and he is supposed to return to England, I may come up with a reason to extend his exile."

Using the royal plural, he said, "We ourself and Bushy, Bagot here, and Green observed Henry Bolingbroke's courtship to the common people — how he seemed to dive into their hearts with humble and familiar courtesy, what reverence he threw away on slaves, wooing poor craftsmen with the craft —

deceit — of smiles and the patient endurance of his fortune, as if to carry their affections into exile with him.

"Off goes his hat to an oyster-wench — a female who sells oysters. A pair of draymen — wagon drivers — bid that God speed him well, and they had the tribute of his supple, easily bending knee, with 'Thanks, my countrymen, my loving friends.' He acted as if he would inherit our England, and as if he were our subjects' next hope to be King."

"Well, he is gone; and with him go these thoughts," Green said. "Now for the rebels who refuse to yield in Ireland. Expeditious management must be made, my liege, before further leisure yield them further opportunities for their advantage and your highness' loss."

"We will ourself go in person to this war," King Richard II said. "And, as for our coffers, with too great a court and liberal largess, they are grown somewhat light, and so we are forced to farm our royal realm."

He had leased out parts of the country to tax-farmers. They paid King Richard II a large sum of money, and then recovered that money — and a profit — by levying their own taxes on the people.

He continued, "The revenue from leasing out the country shall furnish us for our affairs in hand — it shall pay for the war in Ireland. If that revenue falls short, our deputies at home in England shall have blank charters. When my deputies shall know what men are rich, they shall subscribe them for large sums of gold and send the gold to us to supply our wants, for we will make for Ireland soon."

The blank charters were like blank checks. The rich man would sign the blank charter, and the King's deputy would then fill in an amount of money that would be sent to King Richard II.

Bushy entered the room.

"Bushy, what is the news?" King Richard II asked.

"Old John of Gaunt is grievously sick, my lord. He has suddenly taken ill, and he has sent posthaste to entreat your majesty to visit him."

"Where is he staying?"

"At Ely House," Bushy replied.

Ely House was the London palace of the Bishops of Ely; often Ely House was rented out to nobles.

King Richard II said, "Now put it, God, in the physician's mind to help John of Gaunt to his grave immediately! The lining of his coffers shall make coats to deck our soldiers for these Irish wars.

"Come, gentlemen, let's all go visit him. Pray God we may make haste, and come too late!"

Everyone replied, "Amen!"

CHAPTER 2

— 2.1 —

At Ely House, a dying John of Gaunt spoke to the Duke of York, his brother. Attendants were also present.

John of Gaunt said, "Will the King come, so that I may breathe my last while giving wholesome counsel and advice to his unrestrained youth?"

"Don't vex yourself, and don't strive with your breath," the Duke of York said, "because all in vain comes counsel to his ears."

"Oh, but they say the tongues of dying men force others to pay attention as if they were hearing deep harmony and beautiful music. Where words are scarce, they are seldom spent in vain because people who breathe and speak their words in pain breathe and speak truth.

"He who soon must say no more is listened to more than they whom youth and ease have taught to prattle and talk superficially. More are men's ends marked than their lives before: People pay special attention to the dying.

"The setting sun, and music at its close, just like the last taste of sweets, are sweetest because they are last, and they are written in remembrance more than things long past. A person's last words linger longest in the memory of other people.

"Although Richard would not hear my counsel while I was healthy, my death's sad tale may yet undeafen his ears so that he will listen to me."

"No," the Duke of York said. "His ears are stopped with other flattering sounds, such as praises, of whose taste even the wise are fond. His ears are also stopped with lascivious, sexual meters, to whose venomous sound the open ears of youth always listen. In addition, his ears are stopped with reports of fashions in proud Italy, whose manners our apish nation always basely imitates after they are outmoded.

"Where does the world thrust forth a vanity — as long as it is new, no one cares how vile it is — that is not quickly buzzed into King Richard II's ears?

"Then all too late comes counsel to be heard in the place where desires mutiny against reason's considerations.

"Don't try to guide King Richard II because he himself will choose which way he will go.

"It is breath you lack, and that breath you will lose if you try to guide the King with wise counsel."

John of Gaunt replied, "I think that I am a prophet newly inspired, and thus expiring I foretell the King's future. His rash and fierce blaze of riotous and wasteful living cannot last, for violent fires soon burn themselves out.

"Light showers last long, but sudden storms are short.

"A man tires betimes — soon — who spurs his horse too fast betimes — early in the day.

"With eager and hasty feeding, food chokes the feeder.

"Light vanity is frivolous, unthinking pride. It is like an insatiable cormorant — a seabird that gulps its prey. Once it has consumed the resources at its disposal, it soon preys upon itself."

John of Gaunt then began to talk about the British island:

"This royal throne of Kings, this sceptered isle, this earth of majesty, this seat — throne — of the war-god Mars, this other Eden, this demi-paradise, this fortress built by Nature for herself against infection and the hand of war. This happy breed of men, this little world, this precious stone set in the silver sea, which serves it in the role of a wall to keep out invaders, or which serves it as a defensive moat to a house, against the envy and malice of less happier lands. This blessed plot, this earth, this realm, this England, this nurse, this teeming — fertile — womb of royal Kings, feared because of their lineage and famous by their birth, renowned for their deeds as far from home for Christian service in the Crusades and true chivalry as is the Holy Sepulcher in the land of stubborn Jews who rejected Christ, the Holy Sepulcher of the world's ransom, blessed Mary's Son —

"Yes, this land of such dear souls, this dear and again dear land, this land dear for her reputation throughout the world, is now leased out — I die as I say this — as if it were a tenement or a paltry farm.

"England, bound in with — surrounded by — the triumphant sea whose rocky shore beats back the envious siege of watery Neptune, is now bound in with — legally restrained by — shame, with inky blots and rotten parchment bonds, with blank charters and the farming-out of taxes.

"England, which was accustomed to conquer others, has made a shameful conquest of itself.

"Ah, if the scandal would vanish with my life, how happy then would be my ensuing death!"

Several people entered the room: King Richard II, the Queen, the Duke of Aumerle, Bushy, Green, Bagot, Lord Ross, and Lord Willoughby.

The Duke of York said to John of Gaunt, "The King has come. Deal mildly with his youth; for once young hot colts are enraged they rage all the more."

The Queen asked, "How fares our noble uncle, John of Gaunt, the Duke of Lancaster?"

"What comforting thing can you say to me, man?" King Richard II asked. "How is it with aged Gaunt?"

"Oh, how that name 'Gaunt' fits my condition!" John of Gaunt replied. "I am old Gaunt indeed, and I am gaunt through being old. Within me grief has kept a painful fast, and who abstains from food who is not gaunt?

"For sleeping England I have stayed awake and watched a long time. Watching breeds leanness, and leanness is all gaunt. The pleasure that some fathers feed upon is something from which I strictly fast — I mean, the pleasure I would receive from looking at my children. Because Henry Bolingbroke, my son, is in exile, I cannot look upon him.

"And because I am fasting from that pleasure, you have made me gaunt. Gaunt am I for the grave, gaunt as a grave, whose hollow womb inherits and receives nothing but bones since all else has wasted away through fasting."

"Can sick men play so nicely and subtly with their names?" King Richard II asked.

"Misery makes it a sport — an entertainment — to mock itself," John of Gaunt said. "Misery entertains itself by mocking itself.

"Since you seek to kill my name in me by exiling my son, I mock my name, great King, to flatter you."

John of Gaunt was saying that the King had tried to ruin John of Gaunt's family by exiling Henry Bolingbroke, his son, and therefore the King should be pleased when John of Gaunt mocked his own name.

"Should dying men flatter those who live?" King Richard II asked.

"No, no, men who are living flatter those who die," John of Gaunt replied.

"You, who are now dying, say that you are flattering me."

"Oh, no!" John of Gaunt said. "You are dying, although I am sicker than you."

"I am healthy, I breathe, and I see you ill," King Richard II said.

"Now He who made me knows that I see you ill," John of Gaunt said. "Ill in myself to see, and in you seeing ill. I see ill — badly —but I see that you are ill — evil.

"Your deathbed is no lesser than your land — England — wherein you lie sick in reputation. And you, a patient too heedless to take care of yourself, commit your anointed body to the cure of those physicians — flatterers — who first wounded you.

"A thousand flatterers sit within your crown, whose compass is no bigger than your head, and yet, caged in so small a compass, the waste is not a bit less than your land.

"Oh, had your grandfather — King Edward III — with a prophet's eye seen how his son's son should destroy his sons, from out of your reach he would have laid your shame, deposing you before you were possessed of the crown — you who are now possessed by the Devil and acting in such a way as to depose yourself.

"Why, nephew, even if you were regent of the whole world, it would be a shame to lease out this land. Since you don't rule the world but only this land, isn't it more than shame to shame it so by leasing it out?

"You are now the landlord of England, not its King. Your state of law is bondslave to the law. If you were King, you would be the law, but since you are a landlord you are subject to the law and must keep the legal arrangements you have entered into.

"And you —"

King Richard II interrupted, "A lunatic lean- and gaunt-witted fool, presuming on an illness' privilege, you dare with your frozen admonition to make pale our cheek, chasing the royal blood with fury away from its native residence. You are using the excuse of your illness to make me pale with anger.

"Now, by the right royal majesty of my throne, if you were not brother to great King Edward III's son — if you were not the brother of my father, Edward the Black Prince — this tongue that runs so roundly and bluntly in your head should run your head from your disrespectful shoulders. Such speech would get your head chopped off if you were not my uncle."

John of Gaunt replied, "Oh, spare me not, my brother Edward the Black Prince's son, simply because I was the son of his father, King Edward III. That blood, as does the pelican, you have already tapped out like a drink drawn from a tapped barrel and drunkenly consumed as you caroused."

In this culture, the pelican was thought to bite its chest so that its young could drink its blood. This was a metaphor for parental love and filial ingratitude. John of Gaunt was going to accuse King Richard II of spilling King Edward III's blood in the murder of the Duke of Gloucester, one of the sons of King Edward III.

He continued, "My brother the Duke of Gloucester, a plain well-meaning soul, whom may good things befall in Heaven among happy souls, may be a worthy example and good evidence that you have no qualms about spilling King Edward III's blood.

"May you join with the sickness that I now have, and may your unkindness be a scythe that is crooked and bent like old age, so that you may cut down at once a too long withered flower.

"Live in your shame, but may your shame not die with you! May your shame continue after you are dead! May these words hereafter your tormentors be!"

He then said to his attendants, "Convey me to my bed, and then to my grave. People who have love and honor love to live. I receive no love and honor from King Richard II."

John of Gaunt's attendants helped him exit.

King Richard II said, "And let them die who have old age and sullen moods, for you have both, and both are fitting for the grave."

The Duke of York said, "I do beseech your majesty to impute John of Gaunt's words to his perverse sickliness and old age. He loves you, on my life, and he holds you as dear as Harry, Duke of Hereford, were he here."

The Duke of York meant that John of Gaunt loved King Richard II as much as he loved his own son, but Richard II deliberately misinterpreted him to be saying that John of Gaunt loved him as much as his son, Henry Bolingbroke, loved him — that is, not at all.

King Richard II replied, "Right, what you say is true: As the Duke of Hereford loves me, so does John of Gaunt. As their love for me is, so is mine for them, and let all be as it is."

The Earl of Northumberland entered the room and said, "My liege, old Gaunt commends him to your majesty. He conveys his greetings."

"What does he says?" King Richard II replied.

"Nothing; all is said," the Earl of Northumberland said. "His tongue is now a stringless instrument. Words, life, and all, old John of Gaunt, the Duke of Lancaster, has spent. He is dead."

The Duke of York said, "May I, the Duke of York, be the next who must be bankrupt — dead — so! Although the state of death is poor, it ends a mortal woe."

"The ripest fruit first falls, and so does he," King Richard II said. "His time is spent; our pilgrimage through life must also be.

"So much for that.

"Now for our Irish wars. We must get rid of those rough and shaggy-headed lightly armed Irish foot soldiers, who live like venomous snakes where no venomous snakes other than themselves have privilege to live."

According to tradition, Saint Patrick had driven all snakes out of Ireland.

King Richard II continued, "And because these great affairs require some expense, towards our assistance we seize to us the plate, coin, revenues, and moveable possessions that our uncle John of Gaunt possessed."

"How long shall I be patient?" the Duke of York said. "Ah, how long shall tender duty make me tolerate wrong? Not the Duke of Gloucester's death, nor the Duke of Hereford's banishment, nor King Richard II's rebukes and insults to John of Gaunt, nor wrongs done to private individuals in England, nor Richard II's preventing poor Bolingbroke from marrying the cousin of the King of France, nor my own disgrace have ever made me sour my patient cheek, or bend one wrinkle on my sovereign's face. I have never frowned at Richard II, and I have never caused Richard II to frown at me.

"I am the last survivor of noble King Edward III's sons, of whom your father, Edward the Black Prince, the Prince of Wales, was the first and the eldest. In war a lion never raged more fiercely, in peace a gentle lamb was never milder, than was that young and Princely gentleman.

"His face you have, for he looked just like you when he was your age, but when he frowned, it was against the French and not against his friends; his noble hand won what he spent, and he did not spend that which his triumphant father's hand had won. His hands were guilty of no kindred blood; instead, they were bloody with the enemies of his kin.

"Oh, Richard! York — me — is too far gone with grief, or else he never would compare between —"

King Richard II, who had not been paying attention but instead had been looking around, appraising the value of the former possessions of the late John of Gaunt, asked, "Why, uncle, what's the matter?

"Oh, my liege," the Duke of York said, "pardon me, if you please; if you don't please to pardon me, I, who will be pleased not to be pardoned, am content nevertheless.

"Do you seek to seize and grab into your hands the prerogatives and rights of the banished Duke of Hereford? Isn't Gaunt dead, and doesn't Hereford live? Wasn't Gaunt just, and isn't Harry, Duke of Hereford, true and loyal? Didn't the one deserve to have an heir? Isn't his heir a well-deserving son?

"If you take Hereford's rights away, then you take from Time its charters and its customary rights. One time-honored tradition is legal inheritance.

"Unless you respect legal inheritance, then don't let tomorrow follow today. Be not yourself — a King. Why? Because how can you be a King except by fair sequence, progression, and order of succession?

"Now, before God — may God forbid that what I say will become true! — if you wrongfully seize Hereford's rights, if you wrongfully call in and reject all the letters patent that allow him to use those whom he has given his power of attorney to sue and institute proceedings for him to lawfully inherit his father's lands and other possessions, and if you wrongfully deny him the opportunity to offer the homage he would give to you as part of inheriting his father's estate, then you pull down a thousand dangers on your head. You lose a thousand well-disposed hearts and prick my tender patience to think those thoughts that honor and allegiance cannot think."

King Richard II replied, "Think what you will, we seize into our hands his gold- and silverplate, his goods, his money, and his lands."

"I'll not be present for this," the Duke of York said. "My liege, farewell. What will ensue from this action, there's no one who can tell, but we understand that the consequences of bad courses of action can never fall out good."

The Duke of York exited.

King Richard II said, "Go, Bushy, to the Earl of Wiltshire, my Lord Treasurer, straightaway. Tell him to make his way to us at Ely House to see about this business of seizing John of Gaunt's estate. Tomorrow we will make for Ireland, for it is time, I know. And we create, in absence of ourself, our uncle the Duke of York lord governor of England because he is just and has always loved us well.

"Come on, our Queen. Tomorrow we must part. Be merry, for our time of stay is short."

King Richard II, the Queen, the Duke of Aumerle, Bushy, Green, and Bagot exited, leaving behind the Earl of Northumberland, Lord Ross, and Lord Willoughby.

"Well, lords, the Duke of Lancaster is dead," the Earl of Northumberland said.

"And living, too," Lord Ross said, "for now his son is the Duke of Lancaster."

"Barely in title, and not at all in revenue," Lord Willoughby said.

"He would be richly in both, if justice had her right," the Earl of Northumberland said.

"My heart is great," Lord Ross said, "but it must break with silence, before it is disburdened with an indiscreet tongue."

"No, speak your mind," the Earl of Northumberland said, "and let him never speak again who repeats your words to do you harm! If anyone causes you harm by repeating your words, let him never again say anything!"

Lord Willoughby said, "Does what you would speak relate to the Duke of Hereford? If it does, then out with it boldly, man. Quick is my ear to hear of good towards him."

"No good at all can I do for him," Lord Ross said, "unless you call it good to pity him because he is bereft and gelded of his patrimony."

The Earl of Northumberland said, "Now, before God, it is shameful that such wrongs are borne by him, a royal Prince, and by many more of noble blood in this declining land. The King is not himself, for flatterers basely and shamefully lead him; and whatever they will inform him of, merely and purely out of hatred, against any of us, that will the King severely prosecute against us, our lives, our children, and our heirs."

"He has pillaged the common people with grievous taxes, and quite lost their hearts," Lord Ross said. "He has fined the nobles for ancient quarrels, and quite lost their hearts."

"And daily new exactions of exorbitant taxes are devised," Lord Willoughby said, "such as blank charters and forced loans, and I know not what else, but what, in God's name, is done with this money?"

The Earl of Northumberland said, "Wars have not wasted it because King Richard II has not warred. Instead, he shamefully and basely yields upon compromise that which his noble ancestors achieved with blows."

An example of what the Earl of Northumberland was referring to occurred in 1397, when King Richard II surrendered the port of Brest to the Duke of Brittany.

He continued, "King Richard II has spent more money in peace than they in wars."

Lord Ross said, "The Earl of Wiltshire has the realm in farm so he can make money through taxation."

"The King's grown bankrupt, like a broken man," Lord Willoughby said.

"Reproach and dissolution hang over him," the Earl of Northumberland said.

"He has no money for these Irish wars," Lord Ross said, "despite his burdensome taxations, except by robbing the banished Duke of Hereford."

"The Duke of Hereford is his noble kinsman!" the Earl of Northumberland said. "Richard II is a most degenerate King! He is not the man his father and grandfather were! But, lords, we hear this fearful tempest sing, yet we see no shelter in which we can avoid the storm. We see the wind sit sore upon our sails, and yet we strike not, but heedlessly perish because of our overconfidence that we are secure."

The word "strike" was ambiguous. It could mean to strike — lower — one's sails, as in greeting a larger ship or as a defensive maneuver when a sudden squall sprang up. In each case, lowering one's sails was a sign of inferiority. The word "strike" could also mean to strike with weapons against the King. One option was to submit to King Richard II; another option was to rebel against him.

"We see the very wreck that we must suffer," Lord Ross said, "and unavoidable is the danger now because we have been tolerating the causes of our wreck."

"That is not so; the danger is avoidable," the Earl of Northumberland said. "Even through the hollow eyes of death I spy life peering, but I dare not say how near the tidings of our comfort are."

"Let us share your thoughts, as you do ours," Lord Willoughby said.

"Be confident that you can speak freely, Earl of Northumberland," Lord Ross said. "We three are just like you, and if you speak freely to us, your words are like thoughts and will not be heard by anyone else; therefore, be bold and speak freely."

The Earl of Northumberland said, "Then listen to this: I have from Port le Blanc, a bay in Brittany, received news that Harry, the Duke of Hereford; Rainold Lord Cobham; Thomas Arundel, the son and heir of Richard Arundel, who until his beheading in 1397 was the Earl of Arundel — Thomas Arundel recently broke away and escaped from the Duke of Exeter; Richard Arundel's brother, who was recently Archbishop of Canterbury until King Richard II asked the Pope to remove him from that office; Sir Thomas Erpingham; Sir John Ramston; Sir John Norbery; Sir Robert Waterton; and Francis Quoint, all these well furnished by the Duke of Bretagne with eight grand ships and three thousand soldiers of war, are making for England with all due speed and shortly mean to land on our northern shore. Perhaps they would have landed before this, except that they are waiting first for the departure of King Richard II for Ireland.

"If then we shall shake off our slavish yoke, and graft new feathers on our drooping country's broken wing, redeem from the pawnbroker the blemished crown, wipe off the dust that hides our scepter's gilt, and make high majesty look like itself, then go with me posthaste to the port called Ravenspurgh.

"But if you are fainthearted, and are afraid to do so, then stay and keep this secret, and I myself will go."

"Let's go to horse, to horse!" Lord Ross said. "Use your persuasive powers on them who are afraid, not on us!"

Lord Willoughby said, "If my horse holds out, I will be the first one there."

— 2.2 —

The Queen, Bushy, and Bagot spoke together in the palace.

Bushy said to the Queen, "Madam, your majesty is too much downcast. You promised, when you parted from the King, to lay aside life-harming heaviness and depression and to maintain a cheerful disposition."

"To please the King I did promise that," the Queen replied. "To please myself I cannot do it, yet I know no cause why I should welcome such a guest as grief, except that I just bid farewell to so sweet a guest as my sweet Richard.

"Yet again, I think, some unborn sorrow, ready to be born from out of Fortune's womb, is coming towards me, and my inward soul at nothing trembles. At something it grieves, more than with parting from my lord the King."

Bushy said, "Each real grief has twenty shadows, which appear to be grief itself, but they are not so. Sorrow's eye, glazed with blinding tears, divides one thing that is complete in itself into many objects.

"These objects are like perspectives, which rightly gazed upon show nothing but confusion, but when they are eyed awry show clearly and distinctly a form."

Bushy was referring to a kind of picture that when looked at from the front — the usual right way to look at a picture — did not reveal a form. But when looked at from the side, the picture did reveal a form. For example, Hans Holbein the Younger's *The Ambassadors* had a greyish streak at the bottom when looked at from the front, but when looked at from the side, the greyish streak appeared as a human skull.

Bushy continued, "So your sweet majesty, looking awry — mistakenly — upon your lord's departure, finds shapes of grief, more than himself, to bewail. Your lordship's departure, looked on as it is, is nothing but shadows of what it is not."

Here Bushy was referring to another kind of distorted vision. A multiplying glass was one that when looked through would reveal many images. The Queen, looking through her tears at her lord's departure, saw many images of grief although her lord's departure was the one image of grief she should have seen. Her tears performed the function of the multiplying glass.

Bushy continued, "So then, thrice-gracious Queen, do not weep at more than your lord's departure. More grief is not seen, or if it is seen, it is because you are looking with sorrow's false, not genuine, eye, which weeps for imaginary things rather than true things."

The Queen replied, "What you say may be true, but yet my inward soul persuades me that it is otherwise. Whatever the truth may be, I cannot be anything but sad. I am so very sad that although I try to think about nothing, even that nothing makes me very faint and fearful."

"It is nothing but your imagination, my gracious lady," Bushy said.

"It is anything but mere imagination," the Queen said. "Imagination is always derived from some real preceding grief. The grief I feel is not derived from any real preceding grief, for nothing has caused my grief about something, or something has the nothing for which I grieve. The grief is mine because I will inherit it, but what that grief is, that is not yet known to me. I cannot name that grief, and so it is nameless woe, I know."

Green entered the room and said, "God save your majesty! Well met, gentlemen. I hope the King has not yet sailed for Ireland."

"Why do you hope so?" the Queen asked. "It is better to hope that he has sailed for Ireland because his plans need haste, and his haste needs good hope. Why therefore do you hope he has not yet sailed for Ireland?"

Green replied, "So that he, our hope, might pull back his army and keep it in England, and drive into despair an enemy's hope. An enemy has set foot in this land with a strong army. The banished Bolingbroke has himself repealed his sentence of banishment, and with arms brandishing weapons he has safely arrived at the port of Ravenspurgh."

"God in Heaven forbid!" the Queen said.

"Ah, madam, it is too true," Green said, "and what is worse, the Lord Northumberland; the young Henry Percy, Northumberland's son; and the Lords of Ross, Beaumond, and Willoughby, with all their powerful friends, have fled to join him."

Bushy asked, "Why haven't you proclaimed the Earl of Northumberland and all the rest of the rebellious dissident traitors?"

"We have," Green said. "When we did that, the Earl of Worcester broke his staff of office and resigned his stewardship, and all the household attendants — among them many nobles — fled with him to join Bolingbroke."

"So, Green, you are the midwife to my woe," the Queen said. "And Bolingbroke is my sorrow's dismal heir. He is the sorrow to whom I gave birth. Now has my soul brought forth her prodigy, a monster, and I, a gasping newly delivered mother, have woe to woe, sorrow to sorrow joined. Normally, giving birth eases the mother's pains, but since I have given birth to a monster, pain has been added to my pain."

"Don't despair, madam," Bushy said.

"Who shall stop me?" the Queen replied. "I will despair and be at enmity with deceiving Hope. He is a flatterer, a parasite, a keeper back of Death, who gently would dissolve the chains of life — life that false Hope drags out to the utmost degree."

Green said, "Here comes the Duke of York."

The Queen said, "He has signs of war about his aged neck."

The Duke of York was wearing a gorget — armor for the neck. This was sometimes worn with civilian dress to show others that the wearer had military status.

The Queen added, "Oh, full of worried uneasiness are his looks!

"Uncle-in-law, for God's sake, speak comforting words."

"Should I do so, I would belie my thoughts," the Duke of York replied. "Comfort's in Heaven; and we are on the Earth, where nothing lives except crosses and trials, cares and grief. Your husband has gone to keep far-off Ireland under his English rule, while others come to make him lose his land at home.

"Here I am left to prop up his land, although I, weak with age, cannot support myself. I should be a crutch, but I myself need a crutch.

"Now comes the sick hour that King Richard II's surfeit made. He exceeded his royal power, and now he will pay the price. Now he shall put to the test his friends who flattered him."

A servant entered and said to the Duke of York, "My lord, your son was gone before I could reach him."

The Duke of York had wanted his son, the Duke of Aumerle, to come and help him rule England in this time of trouble and rebellion, but his son had gone to Ireland to be with King Richard II.

"He was?" the Duke of York said. "Why, so be it! Let what will happen, happen! Let everything go whichever way it will! The nobles have fled, the commoners are unsympathetic to King Richard II, and they will, I fear, revolt and join the Duke of Hereford's side."

He ordered the servant, "Go to Plashy, to my sister-in-law, the Duchess of Gloucester. Tell her to send me immediately a thousand pounds. Wait, take my ring and show it to her so she knows that you have come to her on my orders."

The servant replied, "My lord, I had forgotten to tell your lordship that earlier today, as I went by her residence, I stopped there — but I shall cause you grief when I report the rest."

"What is it, servant?" the Duke of York asked.

"An hour before I stopped there, the Duchess of Gloucester died."

"May God have mercy!" the Duke of York said. "What a tide of woes comes rushing on this woeful land at once! I don't know what to do. I wish to God, as long as it would not be any disloyalty of mine that had provoked the King to do it, that the King had cut off my head along with the head of the Duke of Gloucester, my brother.

"Are there no messengers dispatched for Ireland? What shall we do for money for these wars?"

He then said to the Queen, "Come, sister-in-law — kinswoman, I should say — please, pardon me."

He was so distracted that he was thinking of the Duchess of Gloucester when he referred to the Queen as his sister-in-law.

He ordered, "Go, servant, get you home and provide some carts and bring away the armor that is there."

Because the household attendants, including many nobles, had fled to join Henry Bolingbroke, the Duke of York planned to use the armor that they had left behind.

The servant exited.

The Duke of York said, "Gentlemen, will you go muster men? If I know how or which way to order these affairs thus thrust disorderly into my hands, never believe me. Both King Richard II and Henry Bolingbroke are my kinsmen. The one is my sovereign, whom both my oath of allegiance and my duty bids me to defend. The other, also my kinsman, is a man whom the King has wronged. Conscience and my relationship to the wronged man bid me to right the wrong done to him.

"Well, we must do something."

He said to the Queen, "Come, kinswoman, I'll make arrangements to take care of you since all the household attendants have deserted."

He then said, "Gentlemen, go, muster up your men, and meet me soon at Berkeley Castle. I should go to Plashy, too, but time will not permit that.

"All is uneven, and everything is left at sixes and sevens. All is in disorder."

The Duke of York and the Queen exited.

Bushy said, "The wind blows west — good for news to go to Ireland. But no ships can return as long as the wind blows west. For us to levy troops commensurate with those of the enemy is entirely impossible."

Green said, "Besides, our nearness to the King in love is near — almost equal to — the hate of those who do not love the King."

Bagot said, "Those who do not love the King are the wavering commoners, for their love lies in their purses, and whoever empties them by so much fills their hearts with deadly hate. They hate the King because of his heavy taxes."

Bushy said, "Because of that, the King stands condemned by everyone."

Bagot said, "If they are the judges, then we also stand condemned because we have always been friends to the King."

Green said, "Well, I will for refuge go immediately to Bristol Castle. The Earl of Wiltshire is already there."

"I will join you," Bushy said. "The commoners, who are full of hate, will perform little service for us, except like dogs to tear us to pieces."

He asked Bagot, "Will you go along with us?"

"No, I will go to Ireland to be with his majesty," Bagot replied. "Farewell. If my heart's forebodings have any meaning, we three who now part shall never meet again."

Bushy said, "That depends on whether the Duke of York can successfully beat back Bolingbroke."

"Alas, the poor Duke of York!" Green said. "The task he undertakes is impossible. It is like counting all the grains of sand and drinking the oceans dry. Where one on his side fights, thousands will flee and desert.

"Farewell at once, for once, for always, and forever."

"Well, we may meet again," Bushy said.

Bagot replied, "I am afraid that we will never meet again."

<h1 style="text-align:center">— 2.3 —</h1>

In the wilds of Gloucestershire, Henry Bolingbroke and the Earl of Northumberland spoke. Soldiers were present.

Henry Bolingbroke asked, "How far is it, my lord, to Berkeley Castle now?"

"Believe me, noble lord, I am a stranger here in Gloucestershire," the Earl of Northumberland replied. "These high wild hills and rough uneven ways draw out and lengthen our miles, and make them wearisome, and yet your fair conversation has been like sugar, making the hard way sweet and delectable.

"But I think to myself what a weary way from Ravenspurgh to the Cotswolds will be found by Ross and Willoughby, who lack your company, which, I protest, has very much beguiled the tedious process of my travel. But their travel is sweetened with the hope to have the present benefit that I possess, and hope to joy is little less in joy than hope enjoyed — the anticipation of enjoying joy is almost as good as the actual enjoyment of joy. With this hope the weary lords shall make their way seem short, as mine has seemed because of the sight of what I have, your noble company."

"Of much less value is my company than your good words," Henry Bolingbroke replied. "But who is coming here?"

Henry Percy, the young son of the Earl of Northumberland, rode up to them.

The Earl of Northumberland said, "It is my son, young Harry Percy, sent from the Earl of Worcester, my brother, wherever he is."

He asked his son, "Harry, how fares your uncle?"

"I had thought, my lord, to have learned about his health from you," young Henry Percy replied.

"Why, isn't he with the Queen?"

"No, my good lord," young Henry Percy replied. "He has forsaken and left the court, broken his staff of office, and dispersed the household attendants of the King."

"What was his reason?" the Earl of Northumberland asked. "He was not so resolved when we last spoke together."

"Because your lordship was proclaimed traitor," young Henry Percy replied. "But he, my lord, has gone to Ravenspurgh, to offer his service to the Duke of

Hereford, and he sent me over by Berkeley, to find out what troops the Duke of York had levied there, and he ordered me to then go to Ravenspurgh."

"Have you forgotten the Duke of Hereford, boy?" his father asked him.

"No, my good lord, for that is not forgotten which never I did remember," young Henry Percy replied. "To my knowledge, I never in my life have seen him."

"Then learn to know him now," his father said, pointing to Henry Bolingbroke. "This is the Duke of Hereford."

To Henry Bolingbroke, young Henry Percy said, "My gracious lord, I tender — offer — you my service, such as it is, being tender, inexperienced, raw, unpolished, and young, which elder days shall ripen and confirm to more approved service and desert. As I grow older, I shall give you better service."

"I thank you, noble Percy," Henry Bolingbroke said, "and be sure that I count myself in nothing else so happy as in a heart that remembers my good friends, and as my fortune — good luck and wealth — ripens with your love, my fortune shall be always your true love's recompense and reward. My heart this covenant makes, and my hand thus seals it."

He shook hands with young Henry Percy.

"How far is it to Berkeley?" the Earl of Northumberland asked. "And what business keeps the good old Duke of York there with his men of war?"

"There stands Berkeley Castle, by yonder thicket of trees," young Henry Percy said. "It is manned with three hundred soldiers, so I have heard, and in it are the Lords of York, Berkeley, and Seymour. No one else of high name and noble rank is there."

Lord Ross and Lord Willoughby rode up to them.

The Earl of Northumberland said, "Here come the Lords of Ross and Willoughby. They are splattered with blood from spurring their horses, and they are fiery-red because of their haste."

"Welcome, my lords," Henry Bolingbroke said to Lord Ross and Lord Willoughby. "I know that you follow a banished traitor — me — because of your good feelings toward me. All my treasury is still only intangible thanks, but when my treasury is more enriched, so shall be the reward for your friendship and labor."

"Your presence makes us rich, most noble lord," Lord Ross said.

"And far surpasses our labor to attain it," Lord Willoughby added.

"'Thanks' is always the treasury of the poor," Henry Bolingbroke said, "and 'thanks' will take the place of my bounty until my infant fortune comes to maturity and I can properly repay you.

"But who is coming here?"

From Berkeley Castle, Lord Berkeley rode up to the group. The Duke of York had sent him to talk to Henry Bolingbroke.

"It is my Lord of Berkeley; that is my guess," the Earl of Northumberland replied.

"My Lord of Hereford, my message is to you," Lord Berkeley said.

Henry Bolingbroke began to speak to Lord Berkeley, but then he decided that Lord Berkeley would have to address him as the Duke of Lancaster first: "My lord, my answer is — address yourself to Lancaster. I have come to seek that name in England, and I must find that title in your tongue, before I make reply to anything you say."

"Mistake me not, my lord," Lord Berkeley said. "It is not my intention to scrape away even one title of your honor. To you, my lord, I come, what lord you will, from the most gracious regent of this land, the Duke of York, to know what pricks you on to take advantage of the King's absence and frighten our native peace with self-borne arms — with weapons carried for your cause and not the country."

The Duke of York, too impatient to wait for Lord Berkeley to return after speaking with Henry Bolingbroke, rode with his attendants over to the group of people.

"I shall not need you to transport my words to the Duke of York," Henry Bolingbroke said. "Here comes his grace in person."

He knelt and said, "My noble uncle!"

"Show me your humble heart, and not your knee," the Duke of York said. "Your knee's duty is deceitful and false and traitorous."

"My gracious uncle —" Henry Bolingbroke began.

"Tut, tut!" the Duke of York interrupted. "Grace me no grace, and uncle me no uncle. I am no traitor's uncle, and that word 'grace' in an ungracious mouth is only profane and blasphemous."

"Ungracious" can mean "lacking in divine grace" and/or "extremely wicked."

The Duke of York continued, "Why have those banished and forbidden legs of yours dared once to touch a speck of dust of England's ground?

"But I have additional questions.

"Why have they dared to march so many miles upon England's peaceful bosom, frightening her pale-faced villagers with war and the display of despised, contemptible arms?

"Did you come because the anointed King is away from England?

"Why, foolish boy, the King is left behind, and in my loyal bosom lies his power. The physical body of the King is in Ireland, but I have the King's authority to govern England in his physical absence."

"Were I only now the lord of such hot youth as I was when your brave father — John of Gaunt — and I rescued Edward the Black Prince, that young war-god Mars of men, from the ranks of many thousand French soldiers, oh, then how quickly should this arm of mine, which is now prisoner to the shaking sickness, chastise you and administer correction to your fault!"

"My gracious uncle, let me know my fault," Henry Bolingbroke replied. "On what condition stands it and wherein? What point of law have I infringed and in what specific way have I infringed it? What personal quality is my fault?"

The word "condition" can mean "point of law" or "personal quality," and Henry Bolingbroke had used both meanings, but the Duke of York used the meaning "circumstance" in his answer.

"Even in condition — the circumstance — of the worst degree: in gross rebellion and detested treason," the Duke of York replied. "You are a banished man, and here you have come before the expiration of your time of banishment, and you are defiantly bearing arms against your sovereign."

"When I was banished, I was banished as Duke of Hereford," Henry Bolingbroke replied, "but now when I come, I come for the title of Duke of Lancaster. And, noble uncle, I beg your grace to look on my wrongs with an impartial eye.

"You are my father, for I think that in you I see old John of Gaunt alive. Oh, then, my father, will you permit that I shall stand condemned to be a wandering vagabond? Will you permit my rights and royal prerogatives to be plucked from my arms by force and given away to upstart spendthrifts?

"Why was I born? If my cousin-King, Richard II, is King of England, it must be granted that I am Duke of Lancaster.

"You have a son, the Duke of Aumerle, who is my noble cousin. If you had died before my father died, and if your son had been trodden down like I have been, your son would have found in his uncle Gaunt a father who would rouse those who did your son wrong and chase them to the bay — a father who would reveal those who wronged your son and chase them to their dying last stand.

"I am denied the opportunity to sue my livery — institute a lawsuit to obtain possession of my lands here — and yet my letters patent legally allow me to do that. My father's goods are all confiscated and sold, and these and all else that ought to be mine are all amiss employed.

"What would you have me do? I am a subject, and I demand my legal rights. The use of attorneys is denied to me, and therefore in person I lay my claim to my inheritance that legally comes to me from my direct descent from my father."

"The noble Duke of Lancaster has been too much abused," the Earl of Northumberland said.

"It is your grace's duty to do the right thing by him," Lord Ross said.

"Base men are made great by his endowments," Lord Willoughby said. "Low-born men have become rich men because they have gotten possession of his inheritance."

"My lords of England, let me tell you this," the Duke of York said. "I have been troubled by my cousin's wrongs and have labored all I could to do him right, but for him to engage in this course of action, to bear defiant arms, to be his own carver — to be his own law — and to cut out his own way to bring about right through the use of wrong, it must not be. And all of you who abet him in this course of action cherish rebellion and are rebels."

"To be his own carver" meant "to carve his own meat" rather than waiting for someone else to carve it. In other words, it meant to help himself to whatever he wanted.

The Earl of Northumberland said, "The noble Duke of Lancaster has sworn his coming is only for what is his own, and for the right of that we all have strongly sworn to give him aid, and let him who breaks that oath never see joy!"

"Well, well," the Duke of York said, "I see the outcome of these arms. I cannot mend it, I must confess, because my army is weak and all left in disorder and without means.

"But if I could, by Him Who gave me life, I would arrest you all and make you stoop unto the sovereign mercy of the King. But since I cannot, let it be known to you I do remain as neuter."

The Duke of York meant that he was neutral between King Richard II and Henry Bolingbroke, but the word "neuter" also meant that he lacked power and effectiveness.

He continued, "So, fare you well, unless you please to enter the castle and repose there this night."

"We will accept that offer, uncle," Henry Bolingbroke said. "But we must win — persuade — your grace to go with us to Bristol Castle, which people say is held by Bushy, Bagot, and their accomplices, the caterpillars — parasites — of the commonwealth. I have sworn to weed the commonwealth and pluck away the caterpillars."

"It may be I will go with you," the Duke of York said, "but yet I'll pause for a while, for I am loath to break our country's laws.

"You are neither my friends nor are you my foes, but to me you are welcome. Things past redress are now with me past care. Past cure, past care."

<h1 style="text-align:center">— 2.4 —</h1>

In a military camp in Wales, the Earl of Salisbury talked with a Welsh Captain.

The Welsh Captain said, "My lord of Salisbury, we have waited for ten days, and with great difficulty kept our countrymen together, and still we hear no tidings from the King; therefore, we will disperse. Farewell."

"Stay yet another day, you trusty Welshman," the Earl of Salisbury requested. "King Richard II reposes all his confidence in you."

"It is thought that the King is dead, so we will not stay. The bay trees — whose evergreen symbolic-of-immortality leaves in Roman days were used to make crowns for victors — in our country are all withered, and meteors frighten the fixed stars of Heaven. The pale-faced Moon looks bloody on the Earth, and lean-faced soothsayers whisper about frightening changes. Rich men look sad and ruffians dance and leap, the one in fear to lose what they possess, the other in hopes to possess those things as a result of violence and war. These signs foretell the death or fall of Kings.

"Farewell. Our Welsh countrymen are gone and fled; they are certain that Richard II their King is dead."

The Welch Captain exited.

The Earl of Salisbury said to himself, "Ah, Richard, with the eyes of heavy, sorrowful mind I see your glory like a shooting star fall to the base, low ground from the sky. Your Sun sets weeping in the lowly west, foreshadowing storms to come, woe and unrest. Your friends have fled to serve your foes, and disadvantageously to your good all fortune goes."

CHAPTER 3

— 3.1 —

Before Bristol Castle, Henry Bolingbroke passed sentence on Bushy and Green, whom he and his men had captured. Also present were the Duke of York, the Earl of Northumberland, Lord Ross, young Henry Percy, Lord Willoughby, and attendants.

"Bring forth these men," Henry Bolingbroke said.

Some attendants brought to him Bushy and Green.

He said, "Bushy and Green, I will not vex your souls — since soon your souls must part from your bodies — with too much convincing you that you have led pernicious lives, for it would not be charitable.

"Yet, to wash your blood from off my hands, here in the view of men I will unfold some of the legal reasons for your deaths.

"You have misled Richard II, a Prince, a royal King, a gentleman fortunate in birth and appearance and qualities. You have made him wholly unfortunate and disfigured.

"You have with your sinful hours made a kind of divorce between his Queen and him, broken the possession of a royal bed, and stained the beauty of a fair Queen's cheeks with tears drawn from her eyes by your foul wrongs.

"I myself, a Prince by fortune of my birth, close to the King by birth, and close to him in friendship until you made him misinterpret me, have stooped my neck and knelt under your injuries, and sighed my English breath up to foreign clouds, eating the bitter bread of banishment, while you have fed upon my signories and estates, used my parks for other than their intended purpose of hunting, felled my forest woods, broken my own stained-glass windows bearing my household coat of arms, and scraped away depictions of my heraldic device, leaving me no sign, except men's opinions and my living blood, to show the world I am a nobleman.

"This, and much more, much more than twice all this, condemns you to die."

He ordered, "See them delivered over to execution and the hand of death."

Bushy said, "More welcome is the stroke of death to me than Bolingbroke is to England. Lords, farewell."

Green said, "My comfort is that Heaven will take our souls and plague unjust men with the pains of Hell. We will enjoy Heaven; you shall suffer Hell."

Henry Bolingbroke ordered, "My Lord Northumberland, see that they are executed."

The Earl of Northumberland and other attendants exited with Bushy and Green.

Henry Bolingbroke said to the Duke of York, "Uncle, you say the Queen is at your house. For God's sake, let her be treated fairly. Tell her I send to her my kind compliments. Take special care that my greetings are delivered."

The Duke of York replied, "A gentleman of mine I have dispatched with a letter fully detailing your friendship to her."

"Thank, gentle uncle," Henry Bolingbroke said.

"Come, lords, away. We must fight against the Welsh leader Glendower and his accomplices. For a while we will work, and afterward we will enjoy holiday."

On the coast of Wales within sight of a castle stood King Richard II. With him were the Bishop of Carlisle, the Duke of Aumerle, and some soldiers.

King Richard II asked, "Do they call this nearby castle Barkloughly Castle?"

"Yes, my lord," the Duke of Aumerle replied. "How does your grace enjoy the air after your recent tossing on the breaking seas as you crossed from Ireland to Wales?"

"I like it well, of course," King Richard II said. "I weep for joy to stand upon my Kingdom once again."

He knelt and touched the ground and said, "Dear earth, I do salute and greet you with my hand, although rebels wound you with their horses' hoofs. Just as a mother long parted from her child plays fondly — affectionately and foolishly — with it and sheds tears and smiles when meeting her child again, so, weeping, smiling, I greet you, my earth, and salute you by touching you with my royal hands.

"My gentle earth, do not feed your sovereign's foe, nor with your fruits comfort his ravenous appetite. Instead, let your poisonous spiders, which suck up venom from you, my earth, and let clumsy-moving poisonous toads lie in their way and injure the treacherous feet that with usurping steps trample you as they take the ground that is yours. Yield stinging nettles to my enemies, and when they from your bosom pluck a flower, guard it, please, with a lurking adder whose forked tongue may with a mortal touch throw death upon your sovereign's enemies.

"Don't mock my imploring of things that lack human sensation, lords. This earth shall have feeling and these stones shall become armed soldiers before her natural King shall falter under foul rebellion's arms."

The Bishop of Carlisle said, "Fear not, my lord. That Power that made you King has the power to keep you King in spite of all. The means that Heaven yields must be embraced, and not neglected; else, if Heaven would, and we will not, Heaven's offer we refuse — we refuse the proffered means of succor and redress. We must make use of the opportunities that Heaven gives us; otherwise, we are rejecting Heaven's help."

The Duke of Aumerle explained to King Richard II, "He means, my lord, that we are too remiss in making use of our opportunities. On the other hand, Henry Bolingbroke, because of our overconfidence, grows strong and great in resources and in troops."

King Richard II replied with a speech in which he compared himself to the Sun. When the Sun shines on the other side of the Earth, it is dark on this side. King Richard II had been away in Ireland, and it had been dark with rebellion in England, but now the King — the metaphorical Sun — had returned to make things light again.

"Disheartening cousin," King Richard II replied, "Don't you know that when the searching eye of Heaven — the Sun — is hidden behind this side of the globe, and lights the lower hemisphere, then thieves and robbers range abroad unseen and commit murders and outrage boldly here. But when from under this terrestrial ball the Sun lights the proud tops of the eastern pines and darts light through every hole where the guilty hide, then murders, treasons, and detested sins, since the cloak of night is plucked from off their backs, stand bare and naked, trembling at the revealing of their crimes and sins?

"So when this thief, this traitor, Bolingbroke, who all this while has reveled in the night while we were wandering with the people in the antipodes — a far-off land — shall see us rising in our throne, the east, his treasons will sit blushing in his face. Bolingbroke will not be able to endure the sight of day, but self-affrighted — afraid as a result of his own actions — will tremble at his sin.

"Not all the water in the rough rude sea can wash the balm — the consecrated oil used in the coronation ceremony — off from an anointed King. The breath of Earthly, mortal men cannot depose the deputy — the King — elected by the Lord.

"For every man whom Bolingbroke has impressed to lift injurious steel against our golden crown, God for his Richard has in Heavenly pay a glorious angel. Then, if angels fight, weak men must fall, for Heaven always guards the right."

The Earl of Salisbury rode up to the group.

King Richard II said, "Welcome, my lord. How far away is your army?"

"Neither nearer nor farther off, my gracious lord, than this weak arm of mine," the Earl of Salisbury replied. "Discouragement guides my tongue and bids me speak of nothing but despair. Your arrival here — one day too late — I am afraid, noble lord, has clouded all your happy days on Earth. Oh, call back yesterday, bid time return, and you shall have twelve thousand fighting men! Today, today, unhappy day, too late, overthrows your joys, friends, fortune, and royal authority. All the Welshmen, hearing that you were dead, have gone to Bolingbroke, dispersed, and fled."

The Duke of Aumerle said to King Richard II, "Take comfort, my liege; why does your grace look so pale?"

"Just now the blood of twenty thousand men triumphed in my face, and they have fled. And, until so much blood thither comes again, don't I have reason to look pale and lifeless?

"All souls who want to be safe fly from my side, for time has set a blot upon my pride."

"Take comfort, my liege," the Duke of Aumerle said. "Remember who you are."

"I had forgotten myself," King Richard II said. "Am I not the King? Awake, you coward majesty! You sleep. Isn't the King's name itself twenty thousand names?

"Arm, arm, my name! A puny subject strikes at your great glory."

He said to the lords with him, "Look not at the ground, you favorites of a King."

Using the royal plural, he added, "Are we not high? High be our thoughts: I know my uncle York has troops enough to serve our turn.

"But who is coming here?"

Sir Stephen Scroop rode over to the group and said, "May more health and happiness befall my liege than can my tongue, which is tuned to the key of sorrow, deliver to him!"

"My ear is open and my heart prepared," King Richard II replied. "The worst you can unfold is worldly loss. Say, is my Kingdom lost? Why, it was my worry and what loss is it to be rid of worry? Does Bolingbroke strive to be as great as we? Greater he shall not be; if he serves God, we'll serve Him, too, and be Bolingbroke's equal in that way. Do our subjects revolt? That we cannot mend. They break their faith to God as well as to us. Even if you proclaim loudly woe, destruction, ruin, and decay, the worst is death, and death will have his day."

"I am glad that your highness is so armed to bear the tidings of calamity," Sir Stephen Scroop said. "Like an unseasonably stormy day, which makes the silver rivers drown their shores, as if the world were all dissolved to tears, so high above his banks swells the rage of Bolingbroke, covering your frightened land with hard bright steel and with hearts harder than steel.

"White-bearded old men have put on helmets and armed their balding and hairless scalps against your majesty. Boys, who still have women's voices, strive to speak forcefully and put their female — weak and delicate — joints in stiff unwieldy armor against your crown. The very beadsmen — old almsmen who are paid to pray for their benefactors — learn to bend their bows of doubly fatal yew against your state."

Yew is doubly fatal because the wood of the yew tree is poisonous and because it is used to make deadly longbows.

Sir Stephen Scroop continued, "Yes, weaving women put down their distaffs in order to wield rusty halberds against your throne. Both young and old rebel, and all goes worse than I have power to tell."

"Too well, too well you tell a tale so ill," King Richard II said. "Where is the Earl of Wiltshire? Where is Bagot? What has become of Bushy? Where is Green? Why have they let the dangerous enemy measure our country's and King's confines with such peaceful steps? Why have they let Bolingbroke travel across the country without opposition? If we prevail, their heads shall pay for it. I am sure that they have made peace with Bolingbroke."

Sir Stephen Scroop made a grim joke: "Peace have they made with him indeed, my lord."

King Richard II said, "Oh, villains, vipers, damned without hope of redemption! Dogs, easily won to fawn on any man! Snakes, in my heart-blood warmed, that sting my heart!"

He was referring to a fable by Aesop: A farmer found a frozen snake. Taking pity on it, he put it under his coat and warmed it. Reviving, the snake, which was venomous, bit him. Dying, the farmer said, "Learn from my example. Don't take pity on scoundrels."

King Richard II continued, "They are three Judases, each one three times worse than Judas, who betrayed Christ! Would they make peace with Bolingbroke? May terrible Hell make war upon their sin-stained souls for this offence!"

Sir Stephen Scroop said, "Sweet love, I see, changing its character, turns to the sourest and most deadly hate. Take back your curse upon their souls; their peace is made with heads, and not with hands. They did not raise their hands to Bolingbroke in greeting, or shake hands with him, or sign a peace treaty. Those whom you curse have felt the worst of death's destroying wounds and lie very low, graved in the hollow ground."

"Are Bushy, Green, and the Earl of Wiltshire dead?" the Earl of Aumerle asked.

"Yes, all of them at Bristol Castle lost their heads," Sir Stephen Scroop replied.

"Where is the Duke of York, my father, with his troops?" the Duke of Aumerle asked.

"It does not matter where," King Richard II said. "Let no man speak of comfort. Let's talk of graves, of worms, and of epitaphs. Let's make dust our paper and with rainy eyes write sorrow on the bosom of the earth. Let's choose executors and talk about wills, and yet let's not do so, for what can we bequeath except our deposed bodies to the ground? Our lands, our lives, and our all are Bolingbroke's, and we can call nothing our own except death and that small model of the barren earth that serves as paste and cover to our bones: we own the flesh that surrounds our bones, and we call our own the ground that will cover our corpses when we are dead.

"For God's sake, let us sit upon the ground and tell sad stories of the death of kings — how some have been deposed, some slain in war, some haunted by the ghosts of those they have deposed, some poisoned by their wives, some killed while sleeping, and all murdered, for within the hollow crown that rounds the mortal temples of a King is the place where Death keeps his court. There the grinning jester — Death — sits, scoffing at the King's splendor and grinning at his pomp, allowing him a breath, a little scene, to play at being a Monarch, and to be feared and to kill with looks. Death infuses the King with the vain conceit of his own self-importance as if this flesh that forms castle walls around our life were impregnable brass. Once Death has amused himself like this, he comes at the last and with a little pin bores through the King's castle wall, and farewell, King!"

As a sign of respect, subjects did not wear hats while in the presence of the King; however, Richard II did not feel much like a King, and so he told his followers, "Cover your heads and don't mock my flesh and blood with solemn reverence. Throw away respect, tradition, form, and ceremonious duty, for you have only mistaken me all this while. I live by eating bread like you, I feel hunger and need, I taste grief, I need friends. Since I am subjected to all this, how can you say to me that I am a King?"

The Bishop of Carlisle said, "My lord, wise men never sit and bewail their woes, but immediately they take steps to thwart the pathways that lead to woe. To fear the foe, since fear oppresses strength, gives in your weakness strength to your foe, and so your follies fight against yourself.

"Fear and be slain; no worse can come by fighting. And to fight and die is death destroying death. If you fight and die, you destroy the power of death by dying. Once you are dead, death has no power over you. In contrast, being afraid of dying pays death servile breath. If you are afraid of dying, you pay Death a servile flattery."

"My father has some troops," the Duke of Aumerle said. "Speak to him, and learn to make a body of a limb. His troops can be the nucleus to which more troops are added."

"You rebuke me well," King Richard II said. "Proud Bolingbroke, I am coming to exchange blows with you for our day of doom — the day that will decide our fate. My ague fit of fear has blown over — an easy task it is to win our own.

"Tell me, Scroop, where is our uncle with his troops? Speak sweetly, man, although your looks be sour."

"Men use the appearance of the sky to judge the state and inclination of the day," Sir Stephen Scroop said. "So may you by my dull and sorrowful eye. My tongue has only a heavier tale to say. I am like a torturer who *slowly* stretches the man on the rack so that he feels more pain. By saying only a little and then a little more, I lengthen the worst that must be spoken.

"Your uncle, the Duke of York, has joined Bolingbroke, and all your northern castles have yielded to Bolingbroke, and all your southern gentlemen have taken up arms in support of Bolingbroke's party."

"You have said enough," King Richard II said.

He then said to the Duke of Aumerle, "Curse you, cousin, who led me away from that sweet way I was in to despair! What do you say now? What comfort do we have now? By Heaven, I'll hate that man everlastingly who bids me to be of comfort any more."

He then said, "Go to Flint Castle. There I'll pine away. A King, woe's slave, shall Kingly woe obey.

"Those troops whom I have, discharge, and let them go to cultivate the land that has some hope to grow, for I have none. I am barren ground, while Bolingbroke is fertile soil.

"Let no man speak again to attempt to get me to alter my decision, for all counsel to me is in vain."

"My liege, one word —" the Duke of Aumerle said.

Richard II interrupted, "He does me double wrong who wounds me with the flatteries of his tongue."

One wound was the raising of false hopes; another was being called "my liege" when it was apparent to Richard II that soon Henry Bolingbroke would be called "my liege."

He added, "Discharge my followers. Let them from here go away, from Richard's night to Bolingbroke's fair day."

Previously, Richard II had compared himself as King to the Sun; now he compared Bolingbroke to the Sun.

Henry Bolingbroke, the Duke of York, and the Earl of Northumberland spoke together before Flint Castle. With them were attendants and troops.

Holding a piece of paper, Henry Bolingbroke said, "We learn from this information that the Welshmen have dispersed, and that the Earl of Salisbury has gone to meet the King, who recently landed with a few private friends upon this coast."

"The news is very fair and good, my lord," the Earl of Northumberland said. "Richard has hidden his head not far from here. He has gone into hiding."

The Duke of York rebuked the Earl of Northumberland: "It would be seemly for the Lord Northumberland to say '*King* Richard.' Feel pity for the sorrowful day when such a sacred King should hide his head."

"Your grace is mistaken," the Earl of Northumberland replied. "I left out his title only in order to be brief."

The Duke of York said, "The time has been, if you would have been so brief with him, he would have been so brief with you as to shorten you, for taking so the head, your whole head's length. If you were to be headstrong and talk that way to the head of state, he would have had you beheaded."

Henry Bolingbroke said, "Don't mistake him, uncle, further than you should. Don't take wrongly what he said."

The Duke of York replied, "Take not, good nephew, further than you should lest you mis-take: The Heavens are over our heads. God is watching us."

The Duke of York was worried that Henry Bolingbroke might unethically take King Richard II's crown.

"I know it, uncle, and I do not oppose myself against the will of Heaven," Henry Bolingbroke said. "But who is coming here?"

Young Henry Percy rode over to the group and said to Henry Bolingbroke, "The castle is royally manned, my lord, against your entrance."

"Royally!" Henry Bolingbroke said. "Why, it contains no King! Or does it?"

"Yes, my good lord," young Henry Percy said, "it does contain a King; King Richard II stays within the limits of yonder castle made of lime and stone, and with him are the Lord Aumerle, Lord Salisbury, Sir Stephen Scroop, besides a clergyman of holy reverence. Who the clergyman is, I cannot learn."

"Oh, probably it is the Bishop of Carlisle," the Earl of Northumberland said.

"Noble lords, go to the rough ribs — the wall — of that ancient castle," Henry Bolingbroke said. "Through the sound of a brazen trumpet, send the breath of parley — a request for a conference — into the ruined ears."

The ruined ears referred to the slits in the castle fortifications, through which archers could shoot arrows. "Ruined ears" also referred to the ears of King Richard II, whom Bolingbroke felt would soon be captured and therefore ruined.

Henry Bolingbroke continued, "Deliver this message:

"Henry Bolingbroke on both his knees kisses King Richard II's hand and sends allegiance and true faith of heart to his most royal person. I, Bolingbroke, have come here to lay my arms and power at Richard II's feet, provided that the King freely grants that my banishment is repealed and my lands are restored again to me.

"If the King will not do this, I'll use the superiority of my power and keep down the summer's dust with showers of blood rained from the wounds of slaughtered Englishmen. But my humble and kneeling duty to the King shall respectfully show how far off from the mind of Bolingbroke is it that such a crimson tempest should drench the fresh green lap of fair King Richard II's land."

He said to the Earl of Northumberland, "Go, tell him that, while here we march upon the grassy carpet of this plain."

He then said, "Let's march — without the noise of threatening military drums — so that from this castle's battered battlements our well-equipped troops may be well seen by the King."

Marching without the sound of drums signified that the troops were not marching to a battle, but Bolingbroke wanted Richard II and his supporters to see that the troops opposing them were superior to any troops the King had.

Bolingbroke continued, "I think that King Richard II and I should meet with no less terror than the elements of fire and water, when their thundering shock at meeting wounds and tears the cloudy cheeks of Heaven."

The word "shock" was used to refer to two soldiers mounted on warhorses charging at each other and fighting each other in battle.

He continued, "If King Richard II is the fire, I'll be the yielding water. Let the rage be his, while on the earth I rain my waters; I will rain them on the earth, and not on him."

By punning — "rain" and "reign" — Bolingbroke was hinting that he would be a better King than Richard II. In his reign, he would metaphorically rain water — so important for abundant crops — on the fields. And by being the water rather than the fire, he was hinting at military supremacy over King Richard II's forces, since lots of water — and Bolingbroke had lots of troops — can put out fire.

He concluded, "March on, and take particular notice of how King Richard II looks."

A trumpet sounded a request for a parle, and from the castle came the sound of an answering trumpet. On the castle walls appeared King Richard II. With him were the Bishop of Carlisle, the Duke of Aumerle, Sir Stephen Scroop, and the Earl of Salisbury.

Henry Bolingbroke said, "See, see, King Richard II himself appears, as does the blushing discontented Sun from out the fiery portal of the east, when he perceives the malicious clouds are bent to dim his glory and to stain the track of his bright passage to the west."

A red Sun in the morning is a sign of a coming storm.

Looking at King Richard II, the Duke of York said, "Yet he looks like a King. Behold, his eye, as bright as is the eagle's, shoots forth controlling majesty like lightning. It would be a pity, a woe, if any harm should stain so fair a show!"

King Richard II stared at the Earl of Northumberland for a few seconds; the Earl of Northumberland did not kneel to the King.

King Richard II said, "We are amazed; and thus long have we stood to watch for the full-of-fear bending of your knee, because we thought ourself your lawful King. And if we are your lawful King, how dare your joints forget to pay their full-of-awe duty to our presence?

"If we are not your lawful King, show us the handwriting of God that has dismissed us from our stewardship; for well we know that no mortal hand of blood and bone can seize the sacred handle of our scepter, unless he profanes, steals, or usurps. To seize our scepter, he would have to be a blasphemer, a thief, or a rebel and usurper.

"And though you think that all, as you have done, have jeopardized their souls by turning them from us, and you think that we are barren and bereft of friends; yet you should know that my master, omnipotent God, is mustering in his clouds on our behalf armies of plague and pestilence, and they shall strike the children who are yet unborn and unbegotten of all you who lift your vassal hands against my head and threaten the glory of my precious crown.

"Tell Bolingbroke — for yonder I think he stands — that every stride he makes upon my land is dangerous treason. He has come to open the bright-red testament of bleeding war, but before the crown he looks for shall live in peace, ten thousand bloody crowns of mothers' sons shall ill become the flower of England's face. Those bloody crowns shall change the complexion of her maiden-pale peace to scarlet indignation and shall bedew her pastor's grass with faithful English blood."

As King of England, Richard II was the pastor — the caretaker — of England.

He added, "Bolingbroke shall have to endure much civil war and many deaths of English young men before he shall wear the crown in peace."

"May the King of Heaven forbid that our lord the King should so with civil and uncivil arms be rushed upon!" the Earl of Northumberland said.

The arms — weapons — would be civil because they were used in civil war; they would be uncivil — uncivilized — because they would be used by Englishmen to kill other Englishmen.

He continued, "Your thrice noble cousin Harry Bolingbroke humbly kisses your hand. He is thrice noble because of his descent from his grandfather King Edward III and from his father, John of Gaunt, and because of his own nobility. And he swears by the honorable tomb, that tomb that stands upon your royal grandsire's bones, the bones of Edward III, and by the royal status of both your bloodlines, currents that spring from one most gracious head, that of Edward III, and by the buried hand of warlike Gaunt, and by the worth and honor of himself, comprising all that may be sworn or said, as I say, on all these things he swears that his coming here has no further scope than to gain what is his by the right of inheritance and to beg for immediate enfranchisement — for his sentence of exile to be revoked — on his knees.

"Once you on your royal part have granted these things, he will hand over his glittering arms to rust, his armored steeds to stables, and his heart to the faithful service of your majesty.

"This he swears, as he is a just Prince. And I believe him, as I am a gentleman."

King Richard II said, "Earl of Northumberland, say that this is the King's answer: The King's noble cousin is very welcome here, and all the number of his fair demands shall be accomplished without contradiction. With all the gracious utterance you have, speak to Bolingbroke's gentle hearing my kind regards."

The Earl of Northumberland left to give King Richard II's answer to Henry Bolingbroke.

King Richard II said to the Duke of Aumerle, "We do debase ourselves, kinsman, do we not, to look so abject and to speak so courteously? Shall we call back the Earl of Northumberland, and send defiance to Henry Bolingbroke, the traitor, and so die?"

"No, my good lord," the Duke of Aumerle replied. "Let's fight with gentle words until time lends us friends, and friends lend us their helpful swords."

"Oh, God! Oh, God!" King Richard II said. "That ever this tongue of mine that laid the sentence of dread banishment on yonder proud man, should take it off again with words of flattery and appeasement! Oh, I wish that I were as great as is my grief, or lesser than my name — my name of King! I wish that I could either forget what I have been, or not remember what I must be now!

"Do you swell, proud heart? Do you beat faster and swell with pride? I'll give you scope — room — to beat, since our foes have scope — opportunity — to beat both you and me."

The Duke of Aumerle said, "The Earl of Northumberland is coming back from talking to Henry Bolingbroke."

"What must the King do now?" King Richard II said. "Must he submit? The King shall do it. Must he be deposed? The King shall be contented. Must he lose the name of King? In God's name, let it go.

"I'll trade my jewels for a set of rosary beads, my gorgeous palace for a hermitage, my gay apparel for an almsman's robe, my embossed goblets for a wooden dish, my scepter for a religious pilgrim's walking staff, my subjects for a pair of carved figures of saints, and my large kingdom for a little grave, a little,

little grave, an obscure grave — or I'll be buried in the King's highway, some way of common passage, where subjects' feet may each hour trample on their sovereign's head; for on my heart they tread now while I am alive, and once I am buried, why shouldn't they trample upon my head?

"Aumerle, you weep, my tender-hearted cousin! We'll make foul weather with despised tears. Our sighs and tears shall flatten the summer corn, and make a dearth of food in this revolting land. Or shall we wantonly play with our woes, and make up some pretty game with shedding tears? For example, we could drop our tears always upon one place, until they have worn away for us a pair of graves within the earth, and there we would be laid with this epitaph: Here lie two kinsmen who dug their graves with weeping eyes. Wouldn't this ill do well? Well, well, I see I talk but idly, and you laugh at me."

He then said to the Earl of Northumberland, "Most mighty Prince, my Lord Northumberland, what does King Bolingbroke say? Will his majesty give Richard permission to live until Richard dies? If you bend your knee to him, Bolingbroke will say yes to whatever you request."

The Earl of Northumberland said, "My lord, in the base court he waits to speak with you. May it please you to come down and talk to him."

The base court was the lower or outer courtyard, sometimes called the servants' courtyard because servants' quarters and stables surrounded it.

King Richard II said, "Down, down I come, like glistening Phaëthon, who borrowed the god Apollo's Sun-chariot and was unable to manage the unruly jades — horses — that pulled it."

In this ancient myth, Phaëthon attempted to drive the Sun-chariot, but he could not manage the horses, and so it came close to Earth and would have set it on fire, but Jupiter, King of the gods, hurled his thunderbolt and killed Phaëthon, who fell to Earth.

He continued, "In the base court? Base court, where Kings grow base, to come at traitors' calls and do them grace. In the base court? Come down? Down, court! Down, King! For night-owls shriek where mounting larks should sing."

Owls are birds of night, while larks are birds of morning. Owls are birds of death and sorrow, while larks are birds of life and joy. Owls swoop low to get their prey, while larks fly high in the sky. Owls shriek, while larks sing beautiful songs. Owls come out when the Sun sets; larks come out when the Sun rises.

As King Richard II and his supporters descended from the high castle walls to the low base court, Henry Bolingbroke asked the Earl of Northumberland, "What does his majesty say?"

"Sorrow and grief of heart make him speak foolishly, like a madman, yet he is coming."

King Richard II and his supporters arrived in the base court.

Henry Bolingbroke ordered those with him to bow to the King: "Stand away from the King, and show fair duty to his majesty."

Henry Bolingbroke knelt and began, "My gracious lord —"

King Richard II interrupted, "Fair cousin, you debase your Princely knee by making the base earth proud by kissing it. I had rather that my heart might feel your love than my unpleased eye see your courtesy."

He pointed to the crown he was wearing and said, "Up, cousin, up; your heart is up, I know, thus high at least, although your knee is low."

"My gracious lord, I come only for what is mine," Henry Bolingbroke replied.

"Your own is yours, and I am yours, and all is yours," King Richard II said.

"Be mine, my most dreaded lord, as far as my true service shall deserve your love," Henry Bolingbroke said.

"You well deserve it," King Richard II said. "They well deserve to have, who know the strongest and surest way to get."

He said to the Duke of York, who was crying, "Uncle, give me your hands. No, don't weep. Dry your eyes. Tears show their love for whom the tears are shed, but tears lack their remedies — they cannot cure what causes them."

He then said to Henry Bolingbroke, "Cousin, I am too young to be your father, although you are old enough to be my heir. What you will have, I'll give to you, and willingly, too, for we must do what force will have us do.

"Shall we set on towards London, cousin? Is that what you want?"

"Yes, my good lord," Henry Bolingbroke replied.

"Then I must not say no," King Richard II replied.

— 3.4 —

In the garden of one of the Duke of York's houses, the Queen and two ladies talked.

The Queen said, "What entertainment shall we devise here in this garden to drive away the gloomy thought of sorrow?"

A lady said, "Madam, we'll play the game of bowls."

"It will make me think the world is full of rubs, and that my fortune rubs against the bias," the Queen said.

Rubs are obstacles that prevent the ball from going where it should. A bias is a weight on one side of the bowl — ball — that makes it curve in a particular direction as it rolls. The Queen's fortune was not going in the direction it ought to go.

"Madam, we'll dance," a lady said.

"My legs can keep no measure — no graceful movement — in delight, when my poor heart keeps no measure — no limit — in grief," the Queen said. "Therefore, no dancing, girl; suggest some other entertainment."

"Madam, we'll tell stories," a lady said.

"Of sorrow or of joy?" the Queen asked.

"Of either, madam," the lady replied.

"Of neither, girl," the Queen said. "For if the stories are of joy, then because I altogether lack joy, they will remind me all the more of sorrow. Or if the stories are of grief, then because I am altogether sad, they will add more sorrow to my lack of joy. For what I have — sorrow — I don't need to repeat, and what I lack — joy — it doesn't help to lament."

"Madam, I'll sing," a lady said.

"It is well that you have cause to sing, but you would please me better if you would weep."

"I could weep, madam, if it would do you good," the lady replied.

"And I could sing, if weeping would do me good, and I would never have to borrow any tear from you," the Queen said. "If weeping would do me good, then much good would be done to me because I have wept so much, and I would be able to sing and I would not need you to weep for me."

A head gardener and two assistant gardeners entered the garden.

Seeing them, the Queen said, "But wait, here come the gardeners. Let's step into the shadow of these trees. I bet all my wretchedness against a row of pins — something trivial — that they'll talk about affairs of state, for everyone does that when they anticipate a political change; woe is forecast by woe."

The Queen and the two ladies moved into the shadows, where they were not seen.

The head gardener said to one assistant, "Go, bind up young dangling apricots, which, like unruly children, make their sire — their father — stoop with oppression of their prodigal and excessive weight. Give some support to and prop up the bending twigs."

He said to the other assistant, "Go, and like an executioner, cut off the heads of too quickly growing sprays — shoots and branches — that look too lofty — tall and overbearing — in our commonwealth. All must be even in our government."

He added, "While you two are thus employed, I will go and root away the noisome, noxious weeds, which without profit and fruit suck the soil's fertility and keep it from wholesome flowers."

An assistant asked, "Why should we within the compass of a fenced-in area keep law and form and due proportion, showing, as in a model, our stable, secure estate, when our sea-walled garden, the whole land of England, is full of weeds, her fairest flowers choked up and suffocated, her fruit trees all upturned, her hedges ruined, her knots — intricately designed flowerbeds — disordered and her wholesome herbs swarming with parasitic caterpillars?"

"Hold your peace and be quiet," the head gardener said. "He who has suffered this disordered spring has now himself met with the fall of leaf — it is his autumn. The weeds that his broad-spreading leaves sheltered — those weeds that ate him while seeming to be holding him up — have been plucked up root and all by Bolingbroke. By 'weeds,' I mean the Earl of Wiltshire, Bushy, and Green."

"Are they dead?" the servant asked.

"They are," the head gardener said, "and Bolingbroke has seized the wasteful King Richard II. Oh, what a pity it is that the King had not so trimmed and tended his land as we trim and tend this garden! We at the correct season wound the bark, the skin of our fruit trees, lest, being overly proud and excessively swollen by sap and blood, with too much riches it confounds and destroys itself. Unless the fruit trees are pruned, the result is excessive wood and lack of fruit.

"Had King Richard II done so to great and growing men, they might have lived to bear fruit and he to taste their fruits of duty. We lop away superfluous branches so that bearing boughs may live. Had King Richard II done so, he himself would bear the crown, which waste of idle, leisure hours has quite thrown down."

"Do you think that the King shall be deposed?" an assistant asked.

"He has already been brought low, and there is fear that he will be deposed," the head gardener said. "A letter came last night to a dear friend of the good Duke of York; the letter tells bad news."

The Queen said, "Oh, I am pressed to death through want of speaking!"

She was referring to a medieval punishment in which suspects who declined to enter a plea of Guilty or Not Guilty in a court of law would have heavy stones placed on them after they lay down. Sometimes, they would continue not to enter a plea, and they would be crushed to death under the weight of stones. People who pled Guilty or who pled Not Guilty and were found guilty and executed had their property forfeited. Sometimes, people refused to enter a plea because they believed that they would be found guilty and would leave their loved ones destitute.

The Queen came out of the shadow of the trees and said to the head gardener, whom she referred to as the likeness of Adam, the first gardener in the first garden, the Garden of Eden, which he shared with Eve, "You, old Adam's likeness, ready to cultivate this garden, how dares your harsh and rude tongue sound and cry out this unpleasing news? What Eve, what serpent, has tempted you to make a second fall of cursed man?"

The first fall occurred when Adam and Eve sinned and God banished them from the Garden of Eden. The head gardener was making a second fall by talking about the likelihood of King Richard II being deposed.

She continued, "Why do you say that King Richard II is deposed? Do you dare, you thing little better than earth, prophesy his downfall? Say where, when, and how you came by these ill tidings! Speak, you wretch."

"Pardon me, madam," the head gardener said. "Little joy have I in telling you this news, yet what I say is true. King Richard II is in the custody of mighty Bolingbroke. Both their fortunes are weighed in a set of scales. In your lord's scale is nothing but himself, and some few vain trifles that make him light, but in the balance of great Bolingbroke, besides himself, are all the English peers, and with that superiority he weighs King Richard II down. If you travel to London, you will find it so. I speak no more than what everyone knows."

The Queen said, "Nimble Mischance, who are so light of foot, doesn't your message belong to me, and yet I am the last who knows it? Oh, you think to serve me last, so that I may the longest keep your sorrow in my breast.

"Come, ladies, go with me to meet at London London's King in woe.

"Was I born to this, that my sad look should grace the triumphal procession of great Bolingbroke?

"Gardener, for telling me this news of woe, I pray to God that the plants you graft may never grow."

The Queen and ladies exited.

The head gardener said, "Poor Queen! So that your state might be no worse, I wish that my skill were subject to your curse.

"Here she let fall a tear; here in this place I'll set a bank of rue, sour herb of grace. Rue, even for ruth — pity, compassion, and sympathy — here shortly shall be seen, in memory of a weeping Queen."

CHAPTER 4

— 4.1 —

In Westminster Hall were meeting Henry Bolingbroke, the Duke of Aumerle, the Earl of Northumberland, young Henry Percy, Lord Fitzwater, the Duke of Surrey, the Bishop of Carlisle, and the Abbot of Westminster. Also present were another lord, a herald, officers, and Bagot.

Henry Bolingbroke ordered, "Call forth Bagot."

Bagot stood forward.

Henry Bolingbroke ordered, "Now, Bagot, freely speak your mind. What do you know about the noble Duke of Gloucester's death? Who wrought it with King Richard II, and who performed the bloody task of his untimely end?"

The word "wrought" meant "worked" or "brought it about." The meaning of that part of the sentence in which the word was used was ambiguous. It could mean "Who brought it about with the King and persuaded him to have the Duke of Gloucester murdered?" or "Who worked with the King to have the Duke of Gloucester murdered?" or both. In September 1397, the Duke of Gloucester had been murdered at Calais.

Bagot replied, "Then set before my face the Lord Aumerle."

Henry Bolingbroke ordered, "Cousin, stand forth, and look upon that man."

Bagot said to the Duke of Aumerle, "My Lord Aumerle, I know your daring tongue scorns to unsay what once it has delivered and stated. In that fatal time when Gloucester's death was plotted, I heard you say, 'Isn't my arm long? It reaches from the restful English court as far as Calais, to my uncle's head.' Among much other talk, at that same time, I heard you say that you would prefer to refuse the offer of a hundred thousand crowns than to have Henry Bolingbroke return to England. You added as well how blest this land would be if your cousin Bolingbroke would die."

The Duke of Aumerle had a higher social status than Bagot. Because of this, if he were challenged to trial by combat he could refuse to fight him on the basis that it would be degrading for him to fight a man of such low rank.

The Duke of Aumerle said, "Princes and noble lords, what answer shall I make to this base man? Shall I so much dishonor my fair stars and high birth to treat him as an equal and give him his punishment? Either I must, or my honor will be soiled by the accusation of his slanderous lips."

He threw down his gage — a gage was an item such as a glove or a hood — as a challenge to combat. They would fight to the death, God would determine the victor, and whichever man still lived would be innocent while the dead man would be guilty.

He said to Bagot, "There is my gage, the manual seal of death, that marks you out for Hell. I say that you lie, and I will maintain that what you have said is false by spilling your heart-blood, although it is all too base to stain the temper and quality of my knightly sword."

Henry Bolingbroke ordered, "Bagot, stand back. You shall not pick up the gage."

Picking up the gage meant accepting the challenge and agreeing to a fight to the death.

The Duke of Aumerle said, "Excepting one person, I wish that the man who had so angered me were the best man and highest ranking among all the men present here."

The one exception was Henry Bolingbroke, whom most of the people present believed would soon be King Henry IV.

Lord Fitzwater threw his gage on the ground and said, "If you say that because your valor insists on fighting only those close to your own rank, then there is my gage, Aumerle, in challenge to your gage.

"By that fair Sun that shows me where you stand, I heard you say, and boastingly you said it, that you were the cause of the noble Duke of Gloucester's death.

"Even if you deny it twenty times, you lie, and I will return your falsehood to your heart, where it was forged, with the point of my rapier."

"You dare not, coward, live to see that day," the Duke of Aumerle said.

"Now by my soul, I wish we could fight during this hour," Lord Fitzwater replied.

"Fitzwater, you are damned to Hell for this," the Duke of Aumerle said.

Young Henry Percy said, "Aumerle, you lie. Fitzwater's honor is as true in this appeal as you are entirely unjust, and that you are so, there I throw my gage, to prove it on you to the extremest point of mortal breathing. I will prove that you are lying by fighting you and taking away your mortal breath. Pick up my gage, if you dare."

"And if I do not, may my hands rot off and never again brandish revengeful steel over the glittering helmet of my foe!" the Duke of Aumerle said, and he picked up the gage.

Another lord said, "I task the earth with a similar burden, falsely swearing Aumerle, and I spur you on with fully as many charges of falsehood as may be hollered in your treacherous ear from sunrise to sunset."

He threw his gage to the ground and said, "There is my honor's pawn — my gage. Pick it up, and engage yourself to a trial by combat, if you dare."

The Duke of Aumerle said, "Who else is betting? By Heaven, I'll throw the dice and bet against all. I have a thousand spirits in one breast and so I can answer twenty thousand such as you."

The Duke of Surrey said, "My Lord Fitzwater, I remember well the exact time that Aumerle and you talked."

"That is very true," Lord Fitzwater replied. "You were present then, and you can witness with me that what I say is true."

"It is as false, by Heaven, as Heaven itself is true," the Duke of Surrey said.

"Surrey, you lie," Lord Fitzwater said.

"Dishonorable boy!" the Duke of Surrey said, throwing down his gage. "That lie shall lie so heavy on my sword, that it shall render vengeance and revenge until you the lie-giver and that lie you told do lie in earth as quietly as your father's skull. In proof of what I say, there is my honor's pawn. Pick it up and engage to meet me in a trial by combat, if you dare."

"How foolishly do you spur a horse that is already eager to run!" Lord Fitzwater said. "If I dare to eat, or drink, or breathe, or live, I dare to meet Surrey in a wilderness, where no one will interfere with the fight, and spit upon him, while I say he lies, and lies, and lies."

He threw down his gage and said, "There is my bond of faith, to tie and commit you to my strong retribution. As I intend to thrive in this new world that Henry Bolingbroke is bringing about, Aumerle is guilty of my true accusation. Besides, I heard the banished Thomas Mowbray, Duke of Norfolk, say that you, Aumerle, sent two of your men to execute the noble Duke of Gloucester at Calais."

"Some honest Christian give me a gage to throw down as I say that the Duke of Norfolk lies," the Duke of Aumerle said.

Someone gave him a gage, and he threw it down and said, "Here I throw this down. If the banishment of the Duke of Norfolk may be repealed, I will try his honor in a trial by combat."

Henry Bolingbroke said, "These differences shall all rest under gage — remain as challenges — until the banishment of the Duke of Norfolk is repealed. Repealed it shall be, and, although he is my enemy, all his lands and estates will be restored to him."

Henry Bolingbroke was taking to himself the power of the King of England. He now used the royal plural: "When the Duke of Norfolk has returned, we will enforce the holding of his trial by combat with the Duke of Aumerle."

The Bishop of Carlisle said, "That honorable day shall never be seen. Many a time has the banished Duke of Norfolk fought for Jesus Christ as a Crusader on a glorious Christian battlefield, flying in the wind the flag of the Christian cross against black pagans, Turks, and Saracens.

"Exhausted with the works of war, he retired to Italy, and at Venice he died and gave his body to that pleasant country's earth, and his pure soul to his Captain — Christ — under whose flag he had fought so long."

"Bishop of Carlisle, is the Duke of Norfolk dead?" Henry Bolingbroke asked.

"As surely as I live, my lord," the Bishop of Carlisle replied.

"May sweet peace conduct his sweet soul to the bosom of good old Abraham!" Henry Bolingbroke said.

He then said to the lords who had thrown down gages and made challenges, "Lords appellants, your differences shall all rest under gage until we assign you to your days of trial."

The Duke of York entered the room, accompanied by attendants.

He said, "Great Duke of Lancaster, Henry Bolingbroke, I come to you from plume-plucked and humbled Richard, who with willing soul adopts you as his heir, and yields his high scepter to the possession of your royal hand. Ascend his throne because as his heir you now descend from him, and long live Henry, fourth of that name!"

"In God's name, I'll ascend the regal throne," Henry Bolingbroke said.

"Mother Mary!" the Bishop of Carlisle said. "God forbid!

"I am only a priest among all you nobles and so I am the lowest-ranking person speaking in this 'royal' presence."

He was sarcastic when he said "'royal' presence." He did not regard Henry Bolingbroke as royalty, although he recognized Henry Bolingbroke as a nobleman.

The Bishop of Carlisle continued, "Yet it may be best fitting for me to speak the truth.

"I wish to God that anyone in this noble presence were noble enough to be the upright judge of noble King Richard II! Then true nobleness would teach him to not commit so foul a wrong as judging the King.

"What subject can give sentence on his King? And who sits here who is not King Richard II's subject? Thieves are not judged except when they are nearby and can hear the trial, even when obvious guilt may be seen in them, and shall the figure — the King — of God's majesty, his captain, steward, deputy-elect, anointed, crowned, planted many years, be judged by subject and inferior breath, and the King himself not present?

"Oh, forbid it, God. Forbid that in a Christian country refined souls and civilized people should do so heinous, black, and obscene a deed!

"I speak to subjects, and I, who am also a subject, speak, stirred up by God, thus boldly for his King.

"My Lord of Hereford here, whom you call King, is a foul traitor to proud Hereford's true King: Richard II."

The Bishop of Carlisle called Henry Bolingbroke "Lord of Hereford," the title he had had when he was exiled. The Bishop did not want to call him "Duke of Lancaster" and especially did not want to call him "King Henry IV."

The Bishop of Carlisle continued, "And if you crown him, let me prophesy what will happen. The blood of Englishmen shall fertilize the ground, and future ages shall groan for this foul act. Peace shall go sleep with Turks and infidels, and in this seat of peace tumultuous wars shall cause kinsmen and fellow-countrymen to confound and destroy each other. Disorder, horror, fear, and mutiny shall inhabit England, and this land shall be called the field of another Golgotha — the place where Christ was crucified as well as a place of dead men's skulls.

"Oh, if you raise this house against this house, it will prove to be the most woeful division that ever fell upon this cursed earth.

"Prevent it, resist it, let it not be so, lest child and child's children cry against you woe!"

The Earl of Northumberland said to the Bishop of Carlisle, "Well have you argued, sir, and for your pains, we here arrest you on a charge of capital treason."

He then ordered, "My Lord of Westminster, it is your charge to safely keep the Bishop of Carlisle until his day of trial."

He continued, "May it please you, lords, to grant the commons' suit." The commons were the commoners.

The commons' suit was a request that the terms of the abdication of King Richard II, who was accused of misgoverning England, be published.

Using the royal plural, Henry Bolingbroke ordered, "Fetch hither Richard, so that in public view he may surrender the throne. That way, we shall proceed without suspicion."

"I will be his escort," the Duke of York said.

He exited.

Henry Bolingbroke said, "Lords, you who here are under our arrest, procure your guarantees that you will show up for your trials. Little are we beholden to your friendship, and we looked for little help from your helping hands."

The Duke of York returned with King Richard II. Some officers carried the crown and other important royal items.

King Richard II said, "Alas, why am I sent for to appear before a King, before I have shaken off the regal thoughts with which I reigned? I hardly yet have learned to ingratiate, flatter, bow, and bend my limbs. Give sorrow permission for a while to tutor me in how to behave in this submission. Yet I well remember the favors — the faces and bows — of these men. Weren't these men mine? Did they not sometimes cry, 'All hail!' to me? So Judas did to Christ, but Christ, who had twelve disciples, found loyalty in all but one. I, with twelve thousand, have found loyalty in none."

He had not yet abdicated the throne, but he was speaking as though he had and as though Henry Bolingbroke were now King Henry IV.

He continued, "God save the King! Will no man say, 'Amen'? Am I both priest and clerk? Well then, amen."

In church services, the priest would say the prayers and the clerk would say, "Amen."

King Richard II continued, "God save the King! Although I am not he, and yet, amen, if Heaven thinks that I am King."

He then asked, "To do what service am I sent for here?"

The Duke of York replied, "To do that office of your own good will that tired majesty — exhaustion caused by ruling England — did make you offer: the resignation of your state and crown to Henry Bolingbroke."

"Give me the crown," King Richard II said.

A lord handed the crown to him, and he said to Henry Bolingbroke, "Here, cousin, seize the crown."

King Richard II chose the word "seize" deliberately.

Henry Bolingbroke hesitated, and King Richard II said impatiently, "Here, cousin."

Henry Bolingbroke laid his hand on the crown, and King Richard II said, "On this side my hand, and on that side yours."

King Richard II now made a comparison in which he referred to a well with two buckets, each tied to one end of the same rope. When a crank was turned, a bucket that was filled with water rose in the air so it could be emptied while the other, empty bucket was lowered into the well water: "Now is this golden crown like a deep well that has two buckets, filling one another, the emptier ever dancing in the air, the other down, unseen and full of water: That bucket down and full of tears am I, drinking my griefs, while you mount up on high."

Henry Bolingbroke said, "I thought you were willing to resign."

"I am willing to resign my crown, but my griefs are still mine. You may depose my glories and my state, but not my griefs. You cannot take them away; I am still King of those."

"Part of your cares you give me with your crown," Henry Bolingbroke said.

In his reply to Henry Bolingbroke, King Richard II used the word "care" in several senses: obligation, responsibility, concern, grief, and worry. Some of these were personal; others related to ruling a country.

King Richard II said, "Your cares set up do not pluck my cares down. My care is loss of care, by old care done. Your care is gain of care, by new care won. The cares I give I have, although they are given away. They are attendant upon the crown, yet still with me they stay."

"Are you contented to resign the crown?" Henry Bolingbroke asked.

King Richard II said, "In reply to your question, I answer this: I, no; no, aye. I must nothing be. Therefore no 'no,' for I resign the crown to you."

He meant this:

"I, no; no, yes.

"I, which sounds like 'aye,' which means 'yes,' means the same thing as a 'no,' since I am nothing now that I have lost my identity as King.

"Since I have lost my identity as King, and since I am nothing, I cannot say 'no' to you, and therefore there is no 'no' — there is only a 'yes,' and I resign the crown to you."

King Richard II paused and then said, "In reply to your question, I answer this: "I know no I. I must nothing be. Therefore no 'no,' for I resign the crown to you."

He meant this:

"I am no longer King because I must resign the crown to you. I am now nothing, a nonentity, and so I cannot know who or what I am.

"Because I am nothing, any reply I can make is meaningless, and so there is no 'no,' and I resign the crown to you."

King Richard II continued, "Now pay careful attention to me and see how I will undo myself."

The word "undo" meant "undress" and "ruin."

He continued, "I give this heavy weight — this crown — from off my head and this unwieldy scepter from my hand and the pride of Kingly power from out my heart. With my own tears I wash away the fragrant oil that was used to anoint me during my coronation. With my own hands I give away my crown. With my own tongue I deny my sacred state. With my own breath I release all oaths and rites of duty and loyalty to me. All pomp and majesty I forswear. My manors, rents, and revenues I forego. My acts, decrees, and statutes I deny. May God pardon all oaths that are broken to me! May God keep all vows unbroken that are sworn to you, Henry Bolingbroke!

"May God make me, who has nothing, be grieved by nothing, and may you be pleased with everything, who have achieved everything!

"Long may you live in Richard's seat to sit, and may Richard soon lie in an earthly pit!

"May God save King Harry, the no-longer-King Richard says, and send him many years of sunshine days!

"What more remains for me to do?"

The Earl of Northumberland said, "No more, except that you read this list of these accusations and these grievous crimes committed by your person and your followers against the state and profit of this land, so that, by hearing you confess them, the souls of men may deem that you are worthily deposed."

"Must I do so?" King Richard II said. "And must I unravel and make clear my weaved-up, intertwined follies? Gentle Northumberland, if your offences were recorded, would it not shame you in so fair a troop of people to read them out loud?

"If you should read them out loud, you would find there one heinous article, containing the deposing of a King and cracking the strong warrant of an oath, marked with a blot, damned in the book of Heaven."

The Earl of Northumberland had sworn an oath of loyalty to King Richard II, who continued, "Nay, all of you who stand here and look at me, while my wretchedness torments me, although some of you, as did Pilate, wash your hands and put on an appearance of pity, yet you Pilates have here delivered me to my bitter cross, and water cannot wash away your sin."

Pontius Pilate ordered that Jesus be crucified.

The Earl of Northumberland said, "My lord, be quick. Read out loud these articles."

King Richard II said, "My eyes are full of tears, I cannot see, and yet salt water does not blind my eyes so much that they cannot see a pack of traitors here. Indeed, if I turn my eyes upon myself, I find that I am a traitor with the rest because I have given here my soul's consent to undeck the ceremonially dressed body of a King, I have made glory base and sovereignty a slave, I have made proud majesty a subject, and I have made splendor a peasant."

"My lord —" the Earl of Northumberland began.

King Richard II interrupted, "I am no lord of yours, you haughty, arrogant, insulting man, nor am I any man's lord. I have no name, no title. No, I don't even have that name that was given to me at the baptismal font — even it has been usurped."

Followers of Henry Bolingbroke were spreading the rumor that King Richard II was a bastard. They said that his real name was Jehan, aka John, and that his father was a priest of Bordeaux, where Richard had been born.

He continued, "Alas, this heavy, sorrowful day. I have worn so many winters out, and I don't now know what name to call myself!

"Oh, I wish that I were a mockery King made of snow, standing before the Sun of Bolingbroke, so I could melt myself away in water-drops!

"Good King, great King, and yet not greatly good, if my word is still sterling — valid and current — in England, let my word command that a mirror be brought here immediately so that it may show me what a face I have, since it is bankrupt of its majesty."

Henry Bolingbroke ordered, "Go some of you and fetch a looking-glass."

An attendant exited to obey the order.

The Earl of Northumberland said to King Richard II, "Read out loud this paper listing your sins and crimes until the mirror is brought here."

"Fiend, you torment me before I arrive in Hell!" King Richard II shouted.

Henry Bolingbroke said, "Leave him alone, my Lord Northumberland."

"The commons — the commoners — will not then be satisfied," the Earl of Northumberland said. "They want his sins and crimes to be publicly announced."

"They shall be satisfied," King Richard II said. "I'll read enough, when I see the very book indeed where all my sins are written, and that's myself — my sins are written in my face."

The attendant returned, carrying a mirror.

King Richard II said, "Give me the looking-glass, and in it I will read what I see."

He looked in the mirror and said, "No deeper wrinkles yet? Has sorrow struck so many blows upon this face of mine, and made no deeper wounds? Oh, flattering looking-glass, similar to my fair-weather followers when I was prosperous, you beguile and deceive me! Was this face the face that everyday under his household roof kept and fed ten thousand men? Was this the face that, like the Sun, made beholders shut their eyes? Was this the face that faced — countenanced — so many follies, and was at last out-faced — discountenanced — by Bolingbroke? A brittle glory shines in this face. As brittle as the glory is the face."

He threw the mirror on the floor, and the mirror shattered.

King Richard II continued, "For there it is, cracked in a hundred slivers. Note carefully, silent King, the moral of this entertainment: How soon my sorrow has destroyed my face."

Henry Bolingbroke said, "The shadow of — the darkness cast by — your sorrow has destroyed the shadow — the image — of your face."

He was contemptuous. King Richard II was acting like a Drama Queen, and Henry Bolingbroke wanted to get the abdication over and done with so he could be King Henry IV.

King Richard II replied, "Say that again. 'The shadow of my sorrow!' Ha!

"Let's see. It is very true that my grief lies all within my soul, and these external manners of laments are merely shadows to the unseen grief that swells with silence in the tortured soul. In my soul lies the substance as opposed to the shadow or appearance, and I thank you, King, for your great bounty that not only gives me cause to wail but also teaches me how to lament the cause.

"I'll beg one boon — favor — from you, and then I will be gone and trouble you no more.

"Shall I obtain the boon I ask for?"

"Name it, fair cousin," Henry Bolingbroke replied.

"'Fair cousin'?" King Richard II said, "I am greater than a King, for when I was a King, my flatterers were then only subjects, but now that I am a subject, I have a King here to be my flatterer. Being so great, I have no need to beg."

"Yet ask me," Henry Bolingbroke said.

"And shall I receive what I ask for?"

"You shall."

"Then give me permission to go."

"To go where?"

"Wherever you want me to go, as long as I am away from your sight and the sight of the others in this room."

Henry Bolingbroke ordered, "Go, some of you convey him to the Tower of London."

"Oh, good!" King Richard II said. "Convey? Conveyers are you all, who rise thus nimbly by a true King's fall."

One meaning of the word "convey" was "steal." King Richard II was saying that these men were thieves — Henry Bolingbroke had stolen the crown and the rest had been his accomplices. Thieves are said to have nimble fingers.

King Richard II, who was soon to be just Richard, exited, accompanied by some lords and a guard.

Henry Bolingbroke, who was soon be King Henry IV, said, using the royal plural, "We solemnly set down Wednesday next as the date of our coronation. Lords, prepare yourselves for it."

Everyone exited except for the Bishop of Carlisle, the Abbot of Westminster, and the Duke of Aumerle.

The Abbot of Westminster said, "We have here beheld a woeful spectacle."

The Bishop of Carlisle said, "The woe's to come; children yet unborn shall feel that this day is as sharp to them as thorn."

The Duke of Aumerle said, "You holy clergymen, is there no plot, no plan, to rid the realm of this pernicious blot?"

The Abbot of Westminster said, "My lord, before I freely speak my mind on that matter, you shall not only take the sacrament and swear on it to keep secret what I intend, but also you will swear to help make happen whatever plot I shall happen to devise.

"I can see that your brows are full of discontent, your hearts of sorrow, and your eyes of tears. Come home with me to supper; and I'll lay before you a plot that shall show us all a happy day."

CHAPTER 5

— 5.1 —

The former Queen — King Richard II had been deposed — and her ladies appeared on a street leading to the Tower of London.

The former Queen said, "This is the way the true King will come; this is the way to the Tower that Julius Caesar began building and that was built for evil ends. Proud Bolingbroke sentenced my condemned lord to be a prisoner in the Tower's flinty bosom.

"Here let us rest, if this rebellious earth has any resting place for her true King's Queen."

Richard, formerly King of England, arrived under guard.

The former Queen said, "But wait a moment, see, or rather do not see, my fair rose wither."

The rose was the King of flowers, just as the lion was the King of beasts.

She continued, "Yet look up, behold, that you — me, myself — in pity may dissolve to dew, and wash him fresh again with true-love tears. Ah, you, Richard, are the ground-plan where old Troy stood."

She was comparing the ruined Richard to the ruin of a city: the city of Troy, famous for its role in the Trojan War. London was sometimes known as Troynovant — New Troy — because a descendant of the Trojan Prince Aeneas was thought to have founded it.

The former Queen continued, "You are the map and image of honor. You are King Richard II's tomb, not King Richard II. You most beauteous inn, why should hard-favored grief be lodged in you, when triumph has become an alehouse guest?"

She was comparing Richard to a beautiful hotel in which Grief was a guest, and Henry Bolingbroke to a common alehouse in which Triumph was a guest.

Richard said to her, "Join not with Grief, fair woman, don't do that because it would make my end too sudden. Learn, good soul, to think our former splendor a happy dream from which we awakened and discovered that the truth of what we are shows us to be only this: I am sworn brother, sweetheart, to grim Necessity, and he and I will maintain an alliance until death.

"Take yourself to France and cloister yourself in some religious house. Our holy lives must win a new world's crown; our profane hours in this world here have struck down our crowns."

The former Queen said, "Is my Richard both in body and mind transformed and weakened? Has Bolingbroke deposed your intellect? Has he been in your heart and taken away your courage? The dying lion thrusts forth its paw, and wounds the earth, if nothing else, with rage at being overpowered. Will you, like a student, take your punishment mildly, kiss the rod, and fawn on rage with base humility when you are a lion and a King of beasts?"

"I am a King of beasts, indeed," Richard said. "The people who deposed me are beasts. If I had been the King of anything but beasts, I would have still been a happy King of men.

"Good, former Queen, prepare yourself to leave for France. Pretend that I am dead and that even here and now you are taking, as from my deathbed, your last living leave of me.

"In winter's tedious nights sit by the fire with good old folks and let them tell you tales of woeful ages that happened long ago; and before you say good night, to requite their tales of griefs tell them the lamentable tale of me and send the hearers weeping to their beds.

"Yes, indeed, the senseless firewood will sympathize with the sorrowful accent of your moving tongue and in compassion weep the fire out. Their resin will seep out like tears. Some pieces of firewood, once burnt, will mourn in ashes, some coal-black, as in wearing mourning clothes, for the deposing of a rightful King."

The Earl of Northumberland and some other men arrived.

The Earl of Northumberland said to Richard, "My lord, Bolingbroke has changed his mind. You must go to Pomfret Castle in Yorkshire, not to the Tower of London."

He then said to the former Queen, "And, madam, arrangements have been made for you. With all swift speed you must go away to your native France."

Richard said, "Earl of Northumberland, you have been the ladder by which the mounting Bolingbroke ascends my throne. The time shall not be many hours older than it is before foul sin gathering head like a boil shall break into corruption and ooze pus. You shall think, even if he were to divide the realm and give you half, it is too little a share for you because you helped Bolingbrook to win it all, and he shall think that you, who know the way to plant unrightful kings on the throne, will know again how to do that. Bolingbroke will think that, for only a very little cause, you will know another way to pluck him headlong from the usurped throne.

"The love that wicked men have for each other turns to fear; that fear then turns to hate, and hate turns one or both wicked men into first being a justifiable danger and then getting a deserved death."

"May my guilt be on my head, and let that be the end to this discussion," the Earl of Northumberland said. "You two take your leave of each other and part from each other; for you must depart quickly."

"Doubly divorced!" Richard said. "Bad men, you violate a twofold marriage: one between my crown and me, and the other between me and my married wife."

He said to his wife, the former Queen, "Let me unkiss the oath of marriage between you and me. And yet we cannot do that, for with a kiss our marriage was made."

He then said, "Part us, Earl of Northumberland; I will go toward the north, where shivering cold and sickness afflicts the region. My wife will go to France, from whence she set forth in pomp. She came to England adorned like sweet May, and she will be sent back to France adorned like Hallowmas — November 1 — or like the shortest day."

The former Queen asked, "And must we be divided? Must we part?"

Richard replied, "Yes, hand from hand, my love, and heart from heart."

The former Queen said to the Earl of Northumberland, "Banish us both and send the King — my Richard — with me."

The Earl of Northumberland said, "That would be a great favor to you, but it would make little sense for us politically."

If Richard and the former Queen were sent to France, they could raise an army and fight a war to get the throne back.

The former Queen said, "Then where he goes, there let me go."

Richard said, "So we two, together weeping, would make one woe. Weep for me in France, and I will weep for you here: Better far off than near, be never the nearer. We might as well be far away from each other than to be near each other and yet never be any closer to seeing each other."

He believed that even if his wife were to stay near him in England, they would not be allowed to see each other.

He continued, "Go, count your way with sighs; I will count my way with groans."

"Then the longest way shall have the longest-lasting moans," the former Queen said.

She had the longer journey to make. Her destination in France was farther distant from London than Pomfret Castle was.

Richard replied, "Twice for one step I'll groan, my way being short, and prolong my way with a heavy heart. Come, come, in wooing sorrow let's be brief, since, wedding it, there is such length in grief. One kiss shall stop our mouths, and in silence we will part."

By kissing each other, they figuratively gave each other their hearts.

He kissed her and said, "Thus I give you my heart, and thus I take your heart."

The former Queen said, "Give me my own heart again; it would be no good part — no good action — for me to keep and kill your heart."

She felt that she would die from sorrow, and that therefore she would kill Richard's heart if she had it when she died.

She kissed him and said, "So, now I have my own heart again, be gone, so that I might strive to kill my own heart with a groan."

She felt that since she had her own heart again, it was OK to die from sorrow — she would be killing with sorrow her own heart, not Richard's.

Richard's final words to her were these: "We make woe wanton and unrestrained with this fond and foolish delay. Once more, adieu; the rest let sorrow say."

The Duke and Duchess of York, aged husband and aged wife, talked together in the Duke of York's palace.

The Duchess of York said, "My lord, you told me you would tell the rest, when weeping made you break the story off, of our two cousins — Richard and Bolingbroke — coming into London."

"Where did I leave off?" the Duke of York asked.

"At that sad stop, my lord, where rude, unruly hands from high windows threw dust and rubbish on King Richard II's head."

"Then, as I said, the Duke of Lancaster, great Henry Bolingbroke, mounted upon a hot and fiery steed that seemed to know his aspiring rider, and with slow but stately pace kept on his course, while all tongues cried, 'God save you, Bolingbroke!'

"You would have thought the very windows spoke, so many greedy looks of young and old through casements darted their desiring eyes upon his visage, and that all the walls with painted imagery had said at the same time, 'Jesus preserve you! Welcome, Bolingbroke!'"

Wall hangings of the time sometimes had word balloons depicting what the figures in the wall hangings — the painted imagery — were saying.

The Duke of York continued, "While he, from the one side to the other turning, bareheaded, bowing lower than his proud steed's neck, spoke to them thus: 'I thank you, countrymen.' And always acting like this, thus he passed along."

"Alas, poor Richard!" the Duchess of York said. "What was his ride like while this was happening?"

"Imagine being in a theater, where the eyes of men, after a talented and popular actor leaves the stage, are idly and indifferently bent on the actor who enters next, thinking his prattle to be tedious. Even so, or with much more contempt, men's eyes scowled at gentle Richard; no man cried, 'God save him!' No joyful tongue gave him a welcome home from Ireland and Wales. But dust was thrown upon his sacred head, which with such gentle sorrow he shook off, his face continually combating with tears and smiles, the badges of his grief and his patience, that had not God, for some strong purpose, steeled the hearts of men, they must necessarily have melted and barbaric people themselves would have pitied him.

"But Heaven has a hand in these events, and to Heaven's high will we submit our calm happiness. To Bolingbroke are we sworn subjects now, whose high position and honor I always will accept."

"Here comes my son, the Duke of Aumerle," the Duchess of York said.

The Duke of York said, "He *was* the Duke of Aumerle, but he lost that title because he was Richard's friend. Richard gave him that title, and the new King took it away. Therefore, madam, you must call him the Earl of Rutland now.

"I am in Parliament the pledge — guarantor — for his loyalty and lasting obedience to the new-made King."

As the pledge of his son's loyalty, the Duke of York would be in danger if his son were to be disloyal to the new-made King. The Duke of York called Bolingbroke "the new-made King" to emphasize that he had been *made* King; he had not inherited the title.

The former Duke of Aumerle walked over to his parents.

"Welcome, my son," the Duchess of York said to him. "Who are the violets now that strew the green lap of the new-come spring? Who are the favorites of the new-come King?"

"Madam, I don't know, nor do I greatly care," the former Duke of Aumerle said. "God knows I should like just as much to be none than one."

"Well, conduct yourself honorably in this new spring of time, lest you be cropped — cut down — before you come to prime," the Duke of York said. "What news is there from Oxford? Will those jousts and tournament still be held there?"

"For anything I know, my lord, they will," the former Duke of Aumerle said.

"You will be there, I know," the Duke of York said.

"Unless God prevents it, I intend to," the former Duke of Aumerle said.

He had a document inside his shirt, but the seal that was attached to the document could be seen.

The Duke of York said, "What seal is that, that is hanging outside your shirt? Do you look pale? Then it must be important. Let me see the document."

"My lord, it is nothing," the former Duke of Aumerle said.

"If it is nothing, then it doesn't matter who sees it," his father said. "You will do what I tell you to do; let me see the document."

"I beg your grace to pardon me. It is a matter of small consequence, which for some reasons I would not have seen."

"Which for some reasons, sir, I mean to see it," his very suspicious father said. "I fear, I fear —"

"What should you fear?" the Duchess of York said. "It is nothing but an IOU for some money he has borrowed to buy gay apparel in preparation for Bolingbroke's triumph day."

"IOU?" the Duke of York said. "An IOU to himself? If he has borrowed money from someone, the other person will be holding the IOU.

"Wife, you are a fool.

"Boy, let me see the document."

His son replied, "I beg you, pardon me; I may not show you the document."

"I will be satisfied," the Duke of York said. "Let me see it, I say."

He grabbed the document and read it. Then he shouted, "Treason! Foul treason! Villain! Traitor! You slave!"

"What is the matter, my lord?" the Duchess of York asked.

"Ho!" the Duke of York said. "Who is within there?"

A servant entered the room.

The Duke of York ordered, "Saddle my horse. I pray to God for His mercy. What treachery is here!"

"Why, what is it, my lord?" the Duchess of York asked.

"Give me my riding boots, I say," the Duke of York ordered the servant. "Saddle my horse."

The servant exited to carry out the orders.

The Duke of York then said, "Now, by my honor, by my life, by my pledged loyalty, I will denounce and inform against the villain."

"What is the matter?" the Duchess of York asked.

"Be quiet, foolish woman," her husband replied.

"I will not be quiet," the Duchess of York replied. "What is the matter, Aumerle?"

"Good mother, be content and calm," the former Duke of Aumerle said. "It is no more than my poor life must answer for."

"Your life answer for!" she said.

"Bring me my riding boots," the Duke of York shouted. "I will ride to the King."

The servant returned, carrying the boots.

"Strike the servant, Aumerle," the Duchess of York ordered. She was frantic and did not want her son to die, and so she was interfering with the servant's attempt to help the Duke of York put on his long riding boots.

The former Duke of Aumerle did not strike the servant.

She said, "Poor boy, you are perplexed and bewildered."

She shouted at the servant, "Go away, villain! Never more come in my sight!"

"Give me my boots, I say," the Duke of York said.

The Duchess of York said, "Why, York, what will you do? Won't you hide the trespass of your own flesh and blood? Have we more sons? Are we likely to have more sons? Haven't my child-bearing years been drunk up by Time? And will you pluck my fair son from my old age, and rob me of a happy mother's name? Doesn't he resemble you? Isn't he your own son?"

"You foolish madwoman," the Duke of York replied, "will you conceal this dark conspiracy? By reading this document, I know that a dozen conspirators have taken the sacrament, put their signatures on a document that each has a copy of, and sworn to kill King Henry IV at Oxford."

"Our son shall not be one of the conspirators," the Duchess of York said. "We'll keep him here, and so then what is the conspiracy to him?"

"Get away from me, foolish woman!" the Duke of York said. "Even if he were twenty times my son, I would still denounce and inform against him."

"If you had groaned for him in childbirth as I have done, you would be more pitiful," the Duchess of York said. "But now I know your mind. You suspect that I have been disloyal to your bed, and that he is a bastard, not your son. Sweet York, sweet husband, don't be of that mind: Don't think that. He is as like you as a man may be. He doesn't resemble me, or any of my kin, and yet I love him."

"Get out of my way, unruly woman!" the Duke of York shouted.

He exited to get on his horse and ride to King Henry IV to inform on the traitors.

"Go after him, Aumerle!" the Duchess of York said. "Get to his horse first, mount it, and ride as quickly as you can and get to the King before he does, and beg your pardon from the King before your father accuses you of treason.

"I will follow. I'll not be long behind; although I am old, I don't doubt that I can ride as fast as York, and I will never rise up from the ground until Bolingbroke has pardoned you. Away, be gone!"

King Henry IV, young Henry Percy, and some other lords talked together in a room at Windsor Palace.

King Henry IV said, "Can't anyone tell me news about my unthrifty, prodigal, and profligate son? It is fully three months since I last saw him. If any plague is hanging over us, it is he. I wish to God, my lords, that he might be found. Inquire at London, among the taverns there, for there, they say, he daily does frequent, with unrestrained loose companions, even such, they say, as stand in narrow lanes, and beat our night watchmen, and rob our wayfarers. He, that spoiled child and unmanly boy, takes as a point of honor to support so dissolute a crew."

The King's prodigal son was known as Prince Hal.

Young Henry Percy said, "My lord, some two days ago I saw the Prince, and I told him about that tournament that will be held at Oxford."

"And what did the 'gallant, fine gentleman' say?" the King asked.

"His answer was, he would go among the brothels, and from the commonest whore pluck a glove, and wear it as a favor — a token of allegiance — and with that he would unhorse the strongest and most robust challenger."

"My son is as dissolute as he is reckless," King Henry IV said, "yet through both bad qualities I see some sparks of better hope, which elder years may happily and hopefully bring forth. But who comes here?"

The former Duke of Aumerle, looking distracted, entered the room and asked, "Where is the King?"

"What does our cousin, who stares and looks so wildly, want?" King Henry IV asked.

"God save your grace!" the former Duke of Aumerle said. "I beg your majesty to allow me to have some conversation alone with your grace."

King Henry IV ordered the others, "Withdraw yourselves, and leave us here alone."

Young Henry Percy and the other lords exited.

King Henry IV asked, "Tell me now, what is the matter with you, our cousin?"

"May my knees forever grow to the earth and my tongue forever cleave to my roof within my mouth unless I receive a pardon before I rise or speak," the former Duke of Aumerle replied.

"Was this fault you want pardoned merely intended, or has it already been committed? Did you merely plan to do it, or have you already committed it? If you merely planned to do it, however heinous it may be, to win your future loyalty I will pardon you."

"Then give me permission to turn the key and lock the door, so that no man may enter until my tale is done."

He wanted to ensure that they were alone when he told the King about the planned assassination.

"You may have your desire," King Henry IV said.

Outside the door, which was now locked, the Duke of York shouted, "My liege, beware; look to defend yourself. You have a traitor in your presence there."

Instantly suspicious of the former Duke of Aumerle, King Henry IV drew his sword and said, "Villain, I'll make you harmless by killing you."

"Stop your revengeful hand; you have no reason to be afraid," the former Duke of Aumerle said.

Outside the door, the Duke of York shouted, "Open the door, you overconfident, foolhardy King. Shall I for love speak treason to your face? I am committing treason by calling you 'foolhardy' because I am so concerned about your safety. Open the door, or I will break it open."

King Henry IV unlocked the door, and the Duke of York entered the room.

"What is the matter, uncle?" King Henry IV said.

Using the royal plural, he added, "Speak. Catch your breath. Tell us how near is danger, so that we may prepare and arm us to encounter it."

The Duke of York handed him the document that he had taken from his son and said, "Peruse this writing here, and you shall learn about the treason that the breathlessness caused by my haste will not allow me to tell you."

The former Duke of Aumerle said to the King, "Remember, as you read, your promise you gave to me. I repent; don't read my name there in that document. My heart is not in league with my signature."

"It was, villain, before your hand set your signature down," the Duke of York said. "I tore the document from the traitor's bosom, King. Fear, and not love, begets the traitor's penitence. Forget your promise to pity him, lest your pity prove to be a serpent that will sting you to the heart."

Reading the document, King Henry IV said, "Oh, heinous, strong, and bold conspiracy! Oh, loyal father of a treacherous son! You pure, immaculate, and silver fountain, from which this stream — your son — through muddy passages has held his current and defiled himself! Your overflow of good transforms to bad in your son, and your abundant goodness shall excuse this deadly blot — sin and signature — of your transgressing son.

"If that happens, then my virtue shall be his vice's pander," the Duke of York said, "and he shall spend my honor with his shame, as thriftless sons spend their scraping, saving fathers' gold.

"My honor lives when his dishonor dies, or my shamed life in his dishonor lies. You kill me by allowing him to live; to save my life, you ought to cause him to die. By your giving him breath, the traitor lives, and the true and loyal man is put to death."

Outside the room, the Duchess of York shouted, "What ho, my liege! For God's sake, let me in."

"What shrill-voiced suppliant makes this eager cry?" King Henry IV asked.

"A woman, and your aunt, great King," the Duchess of York replied. "It is I. Speak with me, pity me, open the door. A beggar is now begging who never begged before."

Recognizing the humor in the situation, King Henry IV said, "Our scene is altered from a serious thing, and it is now changed to a comic scene: 'The Beggar and the King.'"

He said to the former Duke of Aumerle, who was his first cousin, "My dangerous cousin, let your mother in. I know she has come to plead about your foul sin."

The Duke of York said, "If you pardon anyone who asks you for a pardon, more sins may prosper because of your forgiveness. If you cut off this festering limb, the rest of the body politic will rest sound. If you don't treat the festering limb, it can infect all the rest of the body politic."

The Duchess of York entered the room and said, "Oh, King, believe not this hard-hearted man — my husband! Love loving not itself, none other can. If a father doesn't love his son, then he is unable to love anyone, including a King."

The Duke of York said to his wife, "You frantic woman, what are you doing here? Shall your old dugs once more a traitor rear?"

"Sweet York, be patient," the Duchess of York said.

She then said to King Henry IV, "Hear me out, gentle liege."

She knelt.

"Rise up, good aunt," King Henry IV said.

"Not yet, I beg you," she replied. "Forever I will walk upon my knees, and never see a happy day, until you give me joy, until you bid me to be joyful, by pardoning the Earl of Rutland, my transgressing boy."

She knew that it would not be wise to refer to her son as the Duke of Aumerle.

Her son, the former Duke of Aumerle, knelt and said, "In support of my mother's prayers, I bend my knee."

The Duke of York knelt and said, "Against them both my true, loyal joints bended be. Ill may you thrive, if you grant any grace!"

The Duchess of York said, "Do you think that my husband is pleading in earnest? Look at his face: His eyes drop no tears. He pleads to you in jest. His words come from his mouth; our words come from our heart. He pleads only faintly and wants his requests to be denied. We pray with heart and soul and everything else. His weary joints would gladly rise, I know. Our knees shall kneel until to the ground they grow. His prayers are full of false hypocrisy; ours are full of true zeal and deep integrity. Our prayers to you out-pray his; so then let them have that mercy that true prayer ought to have."

"Good aunt, stand up," King Henry IV said.

"No. Do not say 'stand up' to me. Say the word 'pardon' first, and afterwards say 'stand up' to me. If I were your wet nurse, and I were teaching you to talk, 'pardon' would be the first word you would learn to say.

"I never longed to hear a word until now. Say 'pardon,' King; let pity teach you how. The word is short, but it is not so short as it is sweet. No word like 'pardon' is for Kings' mouths so fitting and meet."

The Duke of York said, "Speak it in French, King; say, '*Pardonne moi.*'"

The French words were a polite way of saying no to a request.

The Duchess of York said to her husband, "Do you teach pardon to destroy pardon by using the word against itself? Ah, my sour husband, my hard-hearted lord, you who set the word itself against the word!"

Evil people set the word itself against the word; some evil people even quote the Bible in support of their evil deeds.

She said to King Henry IV, "Speak 'pardon' as it is currently used in our English land. The logic-chopping, meaning-changing French we do not understand. Your eye begins to speak; set your tongue there; or in your piteous heart plant your ear; so that hearing how our lamentations and prayers do pierce, pity may move you to speak the word 'pardon.'"

"Good aunt, stand up," King Henry IV said.

"I do not plead to you in order to stand," the Duchess of York said. "Pardon is all the suit — the petition to you — I have in hand."

"I pardon him, as God shall pardon me," King Henry IV said.

"Oh, happy vantage of a kneeling knee!" the Duchess of York said. "Who would have thought that kneeling would gain a victory! Yet am I sick for fear. Speak that word again. Twice saying the word 'pardon' does not split a pardon in two; instead, it makes one pardon strong."

"With all my heart, I pardon him," King Henry IV said.

"You are a god on Earth," the Duchess of York said.

King Henry IV got serious. Among the conspirators was the Duke of Exeter, his brother-in-law. Also among the conspirators was the Abbot of Westminster.

King Henry IV said, "But as for our 'trustworthy' brother-in-law and the abbot, and all the rest of that conspiring crew of traitors, destruction shall immediately dog them at the heels.

"Good uncle, help to order various forces to go to Oxford, or wherever these traitors are. They shall not live within this world, I swear, without my capturing them, if I once know where they are.

"Uncle, farewell; and, cousin, too, adieu. Your mother well has prayed, and may you prove to be loyal and true."

The Duchess of York said, "Come, my old, degenerate son. I pray that God will make you new."

She wanted her son to reform and be loyal to the new King. She also wanted him to be safe.

Sir Pierce of Exton and a servant talked together in a room of Windsor Castle.

Sir Pierce of Exton said, "Did you notice what words King Henry IV spoke? 'Have I no friend who will get rid of this living fear for me?' Weren't these his words?"

"These were his very words," the servant replied.

"'Have I no friend?' said he. He said it twice, and he emphatically stated it twice together, didn't he?"

"He did."

"And while speaking it, he wistly — intently and longingly — looked at me, as if he wanted to say, 'I wish that you were the man who would divorce this terror from my heart,' meaning King Richard II at Pomfret Castle. Come, let's go. I am King Henry IV's friend, and I will rid him of his foe."

On 14 February 1400, Richard, alone in a room of Pomfret Castle, spoke to himself:

"I have been deliberating how I may compare this prison where I live to the world, but because the world is populous and here there is no creature except myself, I cannot do it; yet I'll puzzle it out, using a hammer to beat things into shape if I must.

"My brain I'll show to be the female to my soul. My soul will be the father; and these two — the female brain and the male soul — will give birth to a generation of continually reproducing thoughts, and these same thoughts will people this little world, this prison I am in. These thoughts will have moods and dispositions like the people of this world, the Earth, for no thought is contented.

"The better sort of thoughts, such as thoughts of things divine, are intermixed with introspective doubts and set the word itself against the word — they set one passage of the Bible against another, seemingly contradictory passage of the Bible.

"For example, 'Come, little ones,' and then again, 'It is as hard to come as for a camel to thread the postern of a small needle's eye.'"

A postern is a little gate.

Matthew 19:14 states, "*Jesus said, 'Suffer the little children [...] to come unto me.'*"

Matthew 19:24 states, "*It is easier for a camel to go through the eye of a needle, than for a rich man to enter into the kingdom of God.*"

The word "camel" also meant "cable-rope," and the word "needle" also meant "door for pedestrians' use in a city gate."

Richard continued, "My most ambitious thoughts plot unlikely wonders, such as how these vain weak fingernails may tear a passage through the flinty ribs — framework — of this hard world, my ragged prison walls, and, because my fingernails cannot, they die in their own pride — they die of frustrated ambition.

"Thoughts leading to happiness flatter themselves that the thinkers are not the first to be slaves to fortune, nor shall they be the last. They are like silly beggars who while sitting in the stocks with their hands and/or feet restrained take refuge from their shame by thinking that many have already and others must in the future sit there in the stocks, and in this thought they find a kind of ease, bearing their own misfortunes on the back of such people as have before endured the same punishment.

"Thus I play in one person many people, and none of those people is contented and happy.

"Sometimes I am King, but then treasons make me wish myself a beggar, and so I am a beggar in my thoughts. Then crushing penury persuades me I was better off when I was a King, and then I am a King again, and by and by I remember that my crown was usurped by Bolingbroke, and immediately I am nothing, but whatever I am, neither I nor any man who is a man shall be pleased by nothing, until he is eased by being nothing. No man is pleased during this life; death brings ease."

Music began to play.

Richard said, "Do I hear music?"

He listened; the music was badly played.

He said, "Ha, ha! Keep time. How sour sweet music is, when time is broken and no proportion kept — when the tempo is broken and no proper rhythm is kept!

"So it is in the music of men's lives, and here in this prison I have the daintiness and sensitivity of ear to rebuke time broken by a disordered stringed instrument. My suffering in prison has made me sensitive to other kinds of disharmony, such as I hear in this music.

"If not for the concord — harmony — of my state and time now, I had not an ear to hear my true situation broken. When I was King — my true situation in life — I paid no attention to the proper conduct of my life, but now that I am no longer King, I can see what I did wrong when I was King. In other words, if not for the peace and quiet of this prison, I would not be able to truly understand the discord in my own affairs when I was King — discord that led to me no longer being King.

"I wasted time, and now Time causes me to waste away, because now Time has made me his numbering clock — a clock with numbers, not a clock that is a sundial.

"My thoughts are minutes, and with sighs they tick, making a discord, and mark their passage on my eyes. My eyes are the outward watch, to which my finger, like the point of a hand on the clock, is always pointing as it cleanses my eyes of their tears. My finger continually wipes away the tears from my eyes."

Still speaking to himself, Richard said, "Now, sir, the sounds that tell the hour are clamorous groans, which strike upon my heart, which is the bell, and so sighs and tears and groans show minutes, quarter-hours and half-hours, and hours, but my time runs quickly on in Bolingbroke's proud joy, while I stand fooling here, his Jack of the clock."

The Jack of a clock is a figurine on top of some clocks that strike the bell and announce the passage of time.

Richard continued, "This music maddens me; let it sound no more because although music has helped madmen to regain their wits, in me it seems it will make wise men mad.

"Yet I ask for a blessing on the heart of the man who gives the gift of music to me! For it is a sign of love, and love given to Richard is a rare jewel in this world of people who hate Richard."

A groom who worked with horses in stables entered the room and said, "Hail, royal Prince!"

"Thanks, noble peer," Richard said. "The cheaper of us is ten groats too dear."

Richard was being courteous when he called the groom, a servant, "noble peer." He was also making a joke when he said, "The cheaper of us is ten groats too dear." The cheaper of the two was Richard because he lacked freedom and was in prison, while the groom was a free man. Richard's joke lay in making a pun on the names of two coins: a royal and a noble. The royal was worth ten groats more than a noble — a groat is a unit of money. Because Richard was no longer royal, he was only a noble, and the groom was valuing him ten groats too dear.

Richard continued, "Who are you? And how did you come here, where no man ever comes but that sad dog — that miserable man — who brings me food to keep me alive and thereby makes my misfortune continue to live?"

His visitor replied, "I was a poor groom of your stable, King, when you were King. I, travelling towards York, with much trouble have finally gotten permission to look upon my former royal master's face.

"Oh, how it grieved my heart when I beheld in London streets, that coronation-day, when Bolingbroke rode on roan Barbary, that horse that you so often have ridden, that horse that I so carefully have groomed!"

"Did Bolingbroke ride on Barbary? Tell me, gentle friend, how went Barbary under Bolingbroke?"

"As proudly as if he disdained to touch the ground."

Richard said, "So proud he was that Bolingbroke was on his back! That jade has eaten food from my royal hand. This hand has made him proud with stroking and petting him. Wouldn't Barbary stumble? Wouldn't he fall down, since pride must have a fall, and break the neck of that proud man who usurped his back?

"I beg your forgiveness, horse! Why do I rant about you, since you, created by God for man to awe, were born to bear? I was not made a horse, and yet I bear a burden like an ass, spurred, chafed, and tired by prancing Bolingbroke."

Holding a dish of food, the jail keeper entered the room.

The jail keeper said to the groom, "Fellow, leave; stay here no longer."

Richard said to the groom, "If you are my friend, it is time you left."

"What my tongue dares not, that my heart shall say," the groom said, and then he exited.

The jail keeper said to Richard, "My lord, will it please you to fall to and eat?"

"Taste my food first, as you are accustomed to do," Richard said.

Someone tasted a King's food before he ate, in case of poison.

The jail keeper said, "My lord, I dare not. Sir Pierce of Exton, who recently came here from the King, commands me not to."

"May the Devil take Henry Bolingbroke — the Duke of Lancaster — and you!" Richard shouted. "Patience is stale, and I am weary of it!"

"Stale" was a strong word; a horse's urine was called "stale."

Richard began to beat the jail keeper, who shouted, "Help! Help! Help!"

Sir Pierce of Exton and some of his men, all of them armed, entered the room.

Richard shouted, "What is this? What is the meaning of Death attacking me in this violent way?"

He grabbed a weapon from one of the men attacking him and shouted, "Villain, your own hand yields the instrument of your death."

He killed the man and shouted, "Go, and fill another room in Hell."

Richard killed another of his attackers, and then Sir Pierce of Exton mortally wounded him.

Richard said, "That hand shall burn in never-quenching fire that made my royal person stagger like this. Exton, your fierce hand has with the King's blood stained the King's own land.

"Mount, mount, my soul, and rise! Your seat is up on high, while my gross flesh sinks downward, here to die."

Richard died.

Sir Pierce of Exton said, "He was as full of valor as of royal blood. Both have I spilled. Oh, I hope that the deed is good! The Devil, who told me I did well, now says that this deed is chronicled in Hell.

"This dead King to the living King I'll bear."

He ordered his men, "Take from here the rest, and give them burial here."

In a room of Windsor Castle, King Henry IV was meeting with the Duke of York. Other lords and some attendants were present.

King Henry IV said, "Kind uncle York, the most recent news we have heard is that the rebels have consumed with fire our town of Cicester in Gloucestershire, but whether the rebels have been captured or slain we have not heard."

The Earl of Northumberland entered the room.

King Henry IV said to him, "Welcome, my lord. What is the news?"

"First, to your sacred chair of state I wish all happiness," the Earl of Northumberland replied. "The most pressing news is, I have to London sent the heads of Oxford, Salisbury, Blunt, and Kent. The manner of their capture is described in detail in this paper here."

"We thank you, gentle Earl of Northumberland and member of the Percy family, for your pains," King Henry IV said. "And to your worth we will add right worthy — well-merited and quite substantial — gains."

Lord Fitzwater entered the room and said, "My lord, I have from Oxford sent to London the heads of Brocas and Sir Bennet Seely, two of the dangerous, conspiring traitors who sought at Oxford your dire overthrow."

"Your pains, Fitzwater, shall not be forgotten," King Henry IV said. "Very noble is your merit, well I know."

Young Henry Percy and the Bishop of Carlisle entered the room.

Young Henry Percy said, "The grand conspirator, the Abbot of Westminster, bearing the burden of conscience and sour melancholy, has died and yielded up his body to the grave. But here is the Bishop of Carlisle, still living and waiting for your Kingly decision and the sentence to punish his pride."

King Henry IV said, "Carlisle, this is your sentence. Choose some secluded place, some monastic dwelling-place that is more sacred than the dwelling-place — the prison cell — you have now, and within it enjoy your life.

"As long as you live peacefully, you will die free from strife, for although you have always been my enemy, yet in you I have seen high sparks of honor."

Sir Pierce of Exton entered the room. Some attendants carried in the coffin that contained Richard's corpse.

Sir Pierce of Exton said, "Great King, within this coffin I present your buried fear. Here in this coffin all breathless lies the mightiest of your greatest enemies, Richard, who was born in Bordeaux, by me brought here."

King Henry IV replied, "Exton, I thank you not; for you have wrought with your fatal hand a deed that will arouse slanderous talk against my head and all this famous land."

"From your own mouth, my lord, I did this deed," Sir Pierce of Exton replied. "You wanted me to kill Richard."

"People who need poison don't love poison," King Henry IV said, "and I don't love you. Although I wished that Richard were dead, I hate the murderer and I love him who was murdered.

"In return for your labor, take a guilty conscience, but you will receive neither my good word nor my Princely favor.

"With Cain, the first murderer, who murdered Abel, go wander through the shadows of night, and never show your head by day or light."

He paused and then said, "Lords, I protest that my soul is full of woe that blood should be sprinkled on me to make me grow.

"Come, mourn with me for that person whom I do lament, and put on sullen black clothing immediately. I'll make a voyage to the Holy Land to wash this blood from my guilty hand.

"March sadly after me; grace my mourning here by weeping after this untimely, premature bier."

Appendix A: Brief Historical Background

KING EDWARD I: 1272-1307

Edward Longshanks fought and defeated the Welsh chieftains, and he made his eldest son the Prince of Wales. He won victories against the Scots, and he brought the coronation stone from Scone to Westminster.

KING EDWARD II: 1307-deposed 1327

At the Battle of Bannockburn in 1314, the Scots defeated his army. His wife and her lover, Mortimer, deposed him. According to legend, he was murdered in Berkeley Castle by means of a red-hot poker thrust up his anus.

KING EDWARD III: 1327-1377

Son of King Edward II, he reigned for a long time — 50 years. Because he wanted to conquer Scotland and France, he started the Hundred Years War in 1338. King Edward III and his eldest son, Edward the Black Prince, won important victories against the French in the Battle of Crécy (1346) and the Battle of Poitiers (1356).

One of King Edward III's sons was John of Gaunt, first Duke of Lancaster.

Another of King Edward III's sons was Edmund of Langley, first Duke of York.

During his reign, the Black Death — the bubonic plague — struck in 1348-1350 and killed half of England's population.

KING RICHARD II: 1377-deposed 1399

King Richard II was the son of Edward the Black Prince. In 1381, Wat Tyler led the Peasants Revolt, which was suppressed. King Richard II sent Henry, Duke of Lancaster, into exile and seized Henry's estates, but in 1399 Henry, Duke of Lancaster, returned from exile and deposed King Richard II, thereby becoming King Henry IV. In 1400, King Richard II was murdered in Pontefract Castle, which is also known as Pomfret Castle.

HOUSE OF LANCASTER

KING HENRY IV: 1399-1413

Henry, Duke of Lancaster, was the son of John of Gaunt, who was the third son of King Edward III. He was born at Bolingbroke Castle and so was also known as Henry of Bolingbroke. Returning from exile in France to reclaim his estates, he deposed King Richard II. He spent the 13 years of his reign putting down rebellions and defending himself against those who would assassinate or depose him. The Welshman Owen Glendower and the English Percy family were among those who fought against him. King Henry IV died at the age of 45.

KING HENRY V: 1413-1422

The son of King Henry IV, King Henry V renewed the war with France. He and his army defeated the French at the Battle of Agincourt (1415) despite being heavily outnumbered. He married Catherine of Valoise, the daughter of the French King, but he died before becoming King of France. He left behind a 10-month-old son, who became King Henry VI.

KING HENRY VI: 1422-deposed 1461; briefly returned to the throne in 1470-1471

The Hundred Years War ended in 1453; the English lost all land in France except for Calais, a port city. After King Henry VI suffered an attack of mental illness in 1454, Richard, third Duke of York and the father of King Henry IV and King Richard III, was made Protector of the Realm. England suffered civil war after the House of York challenged King Henry VI's right to be King of England. In 1470, King Henry VI was briefly restored to the English throne. In 1471, he was murdered in the Tower of London. A short time previously, his son, Edward, Prince of Wales, had been killed at the Battle of Tewkesbury in 1471; this was the final battle in the Wars of the Roses. The Yorkists decisively defeated the Lancastrians.

King Henry VI founded both Eton College and King's College, Cambridge.

WARS OF THE ROSES

From 1455-1487, the Yorkists and the Lancastrians fought for power in England in the famous Wars of the Roses. The emblem of the York family was a white rose, and the emblem of the Lancaster family was a red rose. The Yorkists and the Lancastrians were descended from King Edward III.

HOUSE OF YORK

KING EDWARD IV: 1461-1483 (King Henry VI briefly returned to the throne in 1470-1471)

Son of Richard, third Duke of York, he charged his brother George, Duke of Clarence, with treason and had him murdered in 1478. After dying suddenly, he left behind two sons aged 12 and 9, and five daughters.

His surviving two brothers in Shakespeare's play *Richard III* are these: 1) George, Duke of Clarence. Clarence is the second-oldest brother; and 2) Richard, Duke of Gloucester, and afterwards King Richard III. Gloucester is the youngest surviving brother.

William Caxton established the first printing press in Westminster during King Edward IV's reign.

KING EDWARD V: 1483-1483

The eldest son of King Edward IV, he reigned for only two months, the shortest-lived monarch in English history. He was 13 years old. He and his younger brother, Richard, were murdered in the Tower of London. According to Shakespeare's play, their uncle, Richard, Duke of Gloucester, who became King Richard III, was responsible for their murders.

KING RICHARD III: 1483-1485

Brother of King Edward IV, Richard, the Duke of Gloucester, declared the two Princes in the Tower of London — King Edward V and Richard, Duke of York — illegitimate and made himself King Richard III. In 1485, Henry Tudor, Earl of Richmond, a descendant of John of Gaunt, who was the father of King Henry IV, defeated King Richard III at the Battle of Bosworth Field in Leicestershire. King Richard III died in that battle.

King Richard III's father was Richard Plantagenet, Duke of York. His mother was Cecily Neville, Duchess of York.

King Richard III's death in the Battle of Bosworth Field is regarded as marking the end of the Middle Ages in England.

A NOTE ON THE PLANTAGENETS

The first Plantagenet King was King Henry II (1154-1189). From 1154 until 1485, when King Richard III died, all English kings were Plantagenets. Both the Lancaster family and the York family were Plantagenets.

Geoffrey Plantagenet, Count of Anjou, was the founder of the House of Plantagenet. Geoffrey's son, Henry Curtmantle, became King Henry II of England, thereby founding the Plantagenet dynasty. Geoffrey wore a sprig of broom, a flowering shrub, as a badge; the Latin name for broom is *planta genista*, and from it the name "Plantagenet" arose.

The Plantagenet dynasty can be divided into three parts:

1154-1216: The Angevins. The Angevin Kings were Henry II, Richard I (Richard the Lionheart), and John 1.

1216-1399: The Plantagenets. These Kings ranged from King Henry III to King Richard II.

1399-1485: The Houses of Lancaster and of York. These Kings ranged from King Henry IV to King Richard III.

BEGINNING OF THE TUDOR DYNASTY

KING HENRY VII: 1485-1509

When King Richard III fell at the Battle of Bosworth, Henry Tudor, Earl of Richmond, became King Henry VII. A Lancastrian, he married Elizabeth of York — young Elizabeth of York in *Richard III* — and united the two warring houses, York and Lancaster, thus ending the Wars of the Roses. One of his grandfathers was Sir Owen Tudor, who married Catherine of Valoise, widow of King Henry V.

KING HENRY VIII: 1509-1547

King Henry VIII had six wives. These are their fates: "Divorced, Beheaded, Died, Divorced, Beheaded, Survived." He divorced his first wife, Catherine of Aragon, so that he could marry Anne Boleyn. Because of this, England divorced itself from the Catholic Church, and King Henry VIII became the head of the Church of England. King Henry VIII had one son and two daughters, all of whom became rulers of England: Edward, daughter of Jane Seymour; Mary, daughter of Catherine of Aragon; and Elizabeth, daughter of Anne Boleyn.

KING EDWARD VI: 1547-1553

The son of Henry VIII and Jane Seymour, King Edward VI succeeded his father at the age of nine; a Council of Regency with his uncle, Duke of Somerset, styled Protector, ruled the government.

During King Edward VI's reign, Archbishop Thomas Cranmer wrote the 1549 Book of Common Prayer.

When King Edward VI died, Lady Jane Grey was proclaimed Queen, but she ruled for only nine days before being executed in 1554, aged 17. Mary, daughter of Catherine of Aragon, became Queen. She was Catholic, thus the attempt to make Lady Jane Grey, a Protestant, Queen.

QUEEN MARY I (BLOODY MARY) 1553-1558

Queen Mary I attempted to make England a Catholic nation again. Some Protestant bishops, including Archbishop Thomas Cranmer, were burnt at the stake, and other violence broke out, resulting in her being known as Bloody Mary.

QUEEN ELIZABETH I: 1558-1603

The daughter of King Henry VIII and Anne Boleyn, Queen Elizabeth I was a popular Queen. In 1588, the English navy decisively defeated the Spanish Armada. England had many notable playwrights and poets, including William Shakespeare and Ben Jonson, during her reign. She never married and had no children.

KING JAMES I OF ENGLAND: A MEMBER OF THE HOUSE OF STUART

KING JAMES I OF ENGLAND AND VI OF SCOTLAND: 1603-1625

King James I of England was the son of Mary, Queen of Scots, and Lord Darnley. In 1605 Guy Fawkes and his Catholic co-conspirators were captured before they could blow up the Houses of Parliament; this was known as the Gunpowder Plot.

In 1611, during King James I's reign, the Authorized Version of the Bible (the King James Version) was completed.

Also during King James I's reign, in 1620 the Pilgrims sailed for America in their ship *The Mayflower*.

A NOTE ON SHAKESPEARE

William Shakespeare lived under two monarchs: Queen Elizabeth I and King James I.

Appendix B: About the Author

It was a dark and stormy night. Suddenly a cry rang out, and on a hot summer night in 1954, Josephine, wife of Carl Bruce, gave birth to a boy — me. Unfortunately, this young married couple allowed Reuben Saturday, Josephine's brother, to name their first-born. Reuben, aka "The Joker," decided that Bruce was a nice name, so he decided to name me Bruce Bruce. I have gone by my middle name — David — ever since.

Being named Bruce David Bruce hasn't been all bad. Bank tellers remember me very quickly, so I don't often have to show an ID. It can be fun in charades, also. When I was a counselor as a teenager at Camp Echoing Hills in Warsaw, Ohio, a fellow counselor gave the signs for "sounds like" and "two words," then she pointed to a bruise on her leg twice. Bruise Bruise? Oh yeah, Bruce Bruce is the answer!

Uncle Reuben, by the way, gave me a haircut when I was in kindergarten. He cut my hair short and shaved a small bald spot on the back of my head. My mother wouldn't let me go to school until the bald spot grew out again.

Of all my brothers and sisters (six in all), I am the only transplant to Athens, Ohio. I was born in Newark, Ohio, and have lived all around Southeastern Ohio. However, I moved to Athens to go to Ohio University and have never left.

At Ohio U, I never could make up my mind whether to major in English or Philosophy, so I got a bachelor's degree with a double major in both areas, then I added a master's degree in English and a master's degree in Philosophy.

Currently, and for a long time to come (I eat fruits and vegetables), I am spending my retirement writing books such as *Nadia Comaneci: Perfect 10*, *The Funniest People in Dance*, *Homer's* Iliad: *A Retelling in Prose*, and *William Shakespeare's* Othello: *A Retelling in Prose*.

By the way, my sister Brenda Kennedy writes romances such as *A New Beginning* and *Shattered Dreams*.

Appendix C: Some Books by David Bruce

Retellings of a Classic Work of Literature

Arden of Faversham*: A Retelling*

Ben Jonson's The Alchemist: *A Retelling*

Ben Jonson's The Arraignment, or Poetaster: *A Retelling*

Ben Jonson's Bartholomew Fair: *A Retelling*

Ben Jonson's The Case is Altered: *A Retelling*

Ben Jonson's Catiline's Conspiracy: *A Retelling*

Ben Jonson's The Devil is an Ass: *A Retelling*

Ben Jonson's Epicene: *A Retelling*

Ben Jonson's Every Man in His Humor: *A Retelling*

Ben Jonson's Every Man Out of His Humor: *A Retelling*

Ben Jonson's The Fountain of Self-Love, or Cynthia's Revels: *A Retelling*

Ben Jonson's The Magnetic Lady, or Humors Reconciled: *A Retelling*

Ben Jonson's The New Inn, or The Light Heart: *A Retelling*

Ben Jonson's Sejanus' Fall: *A Retelling*

Ben Jonson's The Staple of News: *A Retelling*

Ben Jonson's A Tale of a Tub: *A Retelling*

Ben Jonson's Volpone, or the Fox: *A Retelling*

Christopher Marlowe's Complete Plays: Retellings

Christopher Marlowe's Dido, Queen of Carthage: *A Retelling*

Christopher Marlowe's Doctor Faustus: *Retellings of the 1604 A-Text and of the 1616 B-Text*

Christopher Marlowe's Edward II: *A Retelling*

Christopher Marlowe's The Massacre at Paris: *A Retelling*

Christopher Marlowe's The Rich Jew of Malta: *A Retelling*

Christopher Marlowe's Tamburlaine, Parts 1 and 2: *Retellings*

Dante's Divine Comedy: *A Retelling in Prose*

Dante's Inferno: *A Retelling in Prose*

Dante's Purgatory: *A Retelling in Prose*

Dante's Paradise: *A Retelling in Prose*

The Famous Victories of Henry V: *A Retelling*

From the Iliad *to the* Odyssey: *A Retelling in Prose of Quintus of Smyrna's* Posthomerica

George Chapman, Ben Jonson, and John Marston's Eastward Ho! *A Retelling*

George Peele's The Arraignment of Paris: *A Retelling*

George Peele's The Battle of Alcazar: *A Retelling*

George Peele's David and Bathsheba, and the Tragedy of Absalom: *A Retelling*

George Peele's Edward I: *A Retelling*

George Peele's The Old Wives' Tale: *A Retelling*

George-a-Greene: *A Retelling*

William Shakespeare's 1 Henry IV, aka Henry IV, Part 1: *A Retelling in Prose*

William Shakespeare's 2 Henry IV, aka Henry IV, Part 2: *A Retelling in Prose*

William Shakespeare's 1 Henry VI, aka Henry VI, Part 1: *A Retelling in Prose*

William Shakespeare's 2 Henry VI, aka Henry VI, Part 2: *A Retelling in Prose*

William Shakespeare's 3 Henry VI, aka Henry VI, Part 3: *A Retelling in Prose*

William Shakespeare's All's Well that Ends Well: *A Retelling in Prose*

William Shakespeare's Antony and Cleopatra: *A Retelling in Prose*

William Shakespeare's As You Like It: *A Retelling in Prose*

William Shakespeare's The Comedy of Errors: *A Retelling in Prose*

William Shakespeare's Coriolanus: *A Retelling in Prose*

William Shakespeare's Cymbeline: *A Retelling in Prose*

William Shakespeare's Hamlet: *A Retelling in Prose*

William Shakespeare's Henry V: *A Retelling in Prose*

William Shakespeare's Henry VIII: *A Retelling in Prose*

William Shakespeare's Julius Caesar: *A Retelling in Prose*

William Shakespeare's King John: *A Retelling in Prose*

William Shakespeare's King Lear: *A Retelling in Prose*

William Shakespeare's Love's Labor's Lost: *A Retelling in Prose*

William Shakespeare's Macbeth: *A Retelling in Prose*

William Shakespeare's Measure for Measure: *A Retelling in Prose*

William Shakespeare's The Merchant of Venice: *A Retelling in Prose*

William Shakespeare's The Merry Wives of Windsor: *A Retelling in Prose*

William Shakespeare's A Midsummer Night's Dream: *A Retelling in Prose*

William Shakespeare's Much Ado About Nothing: *A Retelling in Prose*

William Shakespeare's Othello: *A Retelling in Prose*

William Shakespeare's Pericles, Prince of Tyre: *A Retelling in Prose*

William Shakespeare's Richard II: *A Retelling in Prose*

William Shakespeare's Richard III: *A Retelling in Prose*

William Shakespeare's Romeo and Juliet: *A Retelling in Prose*

William Shakespeare's The Taming of the Shrew: *A Retelling in Prose*

William Shakespeare's The Tempest: *A Retelling in Prose*

William Shakespeare's Timon of Athens: *A Retelling in Prose*

William Shakespeare's Titus Andronicus: *A Retelling in Prose*

William Shakespeare's Troilus and Cressida: *A Retelling in Prose*

William Shakespeare's Twelfth Night: *A Retelling in Prose*

William Shakespeare's The Two Gentlemen of Verona: *A Retelling in Prose*

William Shakespeare's The Two Noble Kinsmen: *A Retelling in Prose*

William Shakespeare's The Winter's Tale: *A Retelling in Prose*